LEGEND
of the
LOST AVENTURINE

HEIDI ENGLISH

This is a work of fiction. Names, characters, places, and incidents are products of the author's imagination or are used fictitiously, and any resemblance to actual persons, living or dead, business establishments, events, or locales is entirely coincidental.

For the daydreamers

A village
  grieves for its soul
its families
  vanished
its houses
  empty
its shops
  deserted
its life
  extinguished
so only ghosts remain.

PROLOGUE

Bruges, Belgium.
April 1499.

"What do you know of the witch's daughter?"

"The witch's ... daughter?" The boy's thin legs quaked as his toes strained to touch the ground. His mind raced as he translated the girl's broken English into his native French.

He'd never heard of the witch's daughter.

"*Oui*, you fool."

There'd been rumors at school of a swirling sorceress who conjured potions from the icy waters of the North Sea.

Maybe she was the witch's daughter.

But that couldn't be it.

No. Certainly not. The boy's father, who was well versed in such things, had dismissed the rumors as rubbish when he'd dared to mention them one winter evening as they warmed themselves by the fire in the parlor.

"Henri," he'd said. "My boy." He leaned in close and caught his son's wide green eyes with his. "I sail the dreaded

North Sea each time I leave you. A fortnight ago I crossed it as I returned from the mighty Rhine River, where rumors flow not of a sorceress, but of a lovely blond maiden called the Lorelei who lures sailors to their deaths upon the jagged rocks."

He paused long enough to tap sweet-smelling tobacco from a worn leather pouch and catch fire to a match on the brick mantle. He puffed into the end of his carved pipe as he swirled the flame across its ivory bowl, briefly illuminating his bearded face.

Only then did he continue, his light eyes twinkling as he met his son's gaze. "I've sailed the North Sea to the great ocean beyond, through the Straits of Gibraltar and the Adriatic Sea to reach the glorious shores of Venice. I can assure you there is not a woman in all of Belgium - sorceress or no - powerful enough to tame those wicked waters."

Clearly his father had not met this girl - this wicked girl - who now held Henri so firmly he was certain he'd never escape.

As if reading his thoughts, she scrunched the rounded folds of his good white collar in her bony fist, lifting him higher until he hovered several inches above the beaten earth.

A gaggle of boys milled nearby on the bank of the canal, watching the proceedings with muted curiosity.

Henri struggled to breath. He wished he'd never wandered back here beyond the red brick brewery on the edge of town. He was certain the girl could see his heart pounding through the woolen flaps of his topcoat.

The air around him sharpened, the hues of earth and sky growing vibrant. The fine details of the girl's thin face etched, unbidden, into his mind.

Pinpoints of light floated into view and hung there, waiting.

He kicked but met only air.

Henri had a dim recollection of seeing the girl before, but he couldn't place where. Her face had been pretty then, not strained with anger and hunger as it was now. Her straw-colored hair, once lush and full, hung limp and dark around her pale face, the long strands brushing the hem of her dirty overcoat.

The canal passed dangerously close to where they stood. Its water ran high and fast from the spring rains and filled the air with the heavy scent of silt and the distant sea.

The sky snapped with the energy of a coming storm. In the distance, narrow ships were moored upstream near the busy Markt, weighed down with goods from far off lands. Bulky shapes moved in the fading light, as the seafaring crews hastened to secure a hard drink and a soft place to sleep before the skies opened. In the tower above them, a heavy bell struck the hour.

Henri's neck burned.

His eyes drifted closed.

The sounds of the evening slowly slipped away.

A hard shake brought him around.

Henri's eyes flew open. He pulled in a deep, ragged breath as the girl eased her grip on his collar.

She began to speak, but somewhere close by a bird wailed, its normal song distorted and panicked.

Henri's eyes darted to locate the source of the sound.

He spotted a dove several yards away.

His heart sank.

The pitiful creature had been snared. Several of the boys surrounded it, ready to play a game he'd heard of but never witnessed firsthand.

The girl gave Henri another rough shake and then dropped him at her feet. His legs crumbled at the surprise release.

He met her dull blue eyes, the dove forgotten.

"The witch's daughter haunts all who tread here," she

warned. "She'll chase you in your dreams until you wake screaming and even your *maman* cannot save you."

Two of the boys broke away from the dove and made their way toward Henri. One was tall with a rat-like face and a gnarled hat. The other was shorter, with blond hair that hung in ringlets across a long forehead.

"Her eyes are dead sockets and she smells of mice and demons," the taller of the two warned, circling Henri and the girl.

"She casts spells that make your skin shrivel and slide from your bones," the other offered, falling in step behind the first.

Laughter traveled across the clearing.

"What do you want me to do with him?" called a boy who stood apart from the others. His low voice cut through the laughter and it ceased.

Henri hadn't noticed him before. He was bigger than the other boys, and older than the girl. He leaned against the canal wall as if bored with the latest turn in their day.

"Bury him like a bird," a lanky boy called from across the clearing before picking up a heavy stone from the ground. He tossed it into the air to feel its weight. Henri looked away, unable to watch what he feared would happen next.

The dove stilled, cried out, and began to screech again.

At the dove's cry, Henri scrambled backward to his feet and, remembering his station for the first time since wandering into this nest of ne'er-do-wells, puffed his chest and raised his chin.

He was younger than the children who surrounded him, but he was a LeFort and, even here, he knew that meant something.

Across the clearing, the dove's cries fell silent.

The girl leaned in, her breath hot on his face.

"*Cours,*" she whispered in French. Then, in translation,

"Run."

Henri blinked.

He didn't know what he expected but it wasn't that.

He took a half step back, then bolted up the dirt path toward the Minnewater park, where the open iron gates would grant his freedom on the busy cobblestone lanes beyond.

A few of the boys snickered as they watched him run away.

"Surprised he didn't pass out," one said, to which the other boys gave a hearty laugh, all but the biggest one who peeled himself away from the canal wall to stand in front of the girl.

"And if he tells?"

She scoffed. "Tells what? Tells whom? His own hide would be in greater danger than ours if his *maman* discovered he was here with the likes of us."

"Do you know him, Eva?" the rat-faced boy asked, taking a place beside her.

She nodded, watching the small figure draw away and disappear beyond the gate. "His father is an Alderman."

The older boy shrugged, unimpressed.

"Come on, Jan," the rock-thrower called to him from across the clearing. "I see another bird."

In the Middle Ages, Bruges
(pronounced *broojz*) was the
richest city in Belgium, with
a thriving port that welcomed
merchants from across the known
world and a hopping market square
that rivaled only Venice. But by the 1500s
Bruges was all but abandoned and forgotten.
It remained that way, a mysterious time capsule
near the sea, until tourists rediscovered
its charms in the romantic age.

Marty McEntire's
Europe for Americans Travel Guide

CHAPTER ONE

Bruges, Belgium.
Present day.

Birdie Blessing followed her mother through shimmering cobblestone lanes at twilight on the longest day of the year. They were running late, having missed their connecting train to Bruges at the sprawling station in Brussels.

"A few more blocks," Mrs. Blessing called over her shoulder as a solitary bell in a tower somewhere high above them tolled.

Fifteen-year old Birdie tugged her suitcase behind her, its wheels bumping on the uneven stones. For the third time in as many minutes the purple case tilted to the right, twisting her slim wrist with it. As she attempted to right the uncooperative piece of luggage, the thick straps of her matching backpack slipped from her slender shoulders.

"Come on, Birdie," Mrs. Blessing said, somehow knowing she'd stopped without turning around to check. "We don't have much time."

The bell tolled again, then quieted as the deep note

faded into the night.

Birdie yanked the straps of her backpack, tightening them more than usual, and reclaimed her suitcase handle.

I wish Jonah were here, she thought as the pack's weight pulled at her shoulders.

Her eyes began to sting.

No.

She took a deep breath in the fading light and deliberately pushed the thought away. She could not think about her brother right now.

The bell tolled again.

Was that three times? Or had she missed one?

She checked her watch.

9:49 pm.

Why was the stupid bell ringing at all?

"Birdie?"

She started off again, hurrying on long legs to catch up to her mother, who by now had pulled several yards ahead. She fell into step behind her.

From time to time Birdie dared to lift her eyes from her footing long enough to marvel at the grand facades of the Gothic buildings that leaned heavily against each other in the deepening light, each dependent on the next for support after centuries of standing together. The buildings rose in shades of burgundy, beige, and gray until they reached their elaborate roofs, where carvings and painted edging transformed them into a scene from a fairy tale.

There was something else, too, about the beautiful buildings that encircled them: a sensation of being watched that she'd prayed would fall away as they flew thousands of miles across the ocean, high above the clouds.

But the shadows were here, too, in every window, questioning them as they made their way alone through the quiet back streets.

Birdie's sneaker caught the edge of a cobblestone and she

tumbled forward, catching herself with her free hand before she crashed onto the lane.

She stood up, adjusted her luggage, and refocused on her footing.

"I am in no danger here," she whispered. She squeezed her eyes closed, trying to believe it.

"What did you say, Birdie?"

"Nothing."

She opened her eyes, and flicked a piece of gravel from the heel of her palm. She loosened the tie that held her long chestnut hair and it fell in a wave that warmed her back and screened her pale face from unwanted eyes.

The bell struck its last note by the time they reached a small square where half-a-dozen cobbled lanes and alleys converged. Mrs. Blessing paused to study the map she'd printed at home before both the printer and the computer had been tucked into moving boxes.

"Are we lost?" Birdie asked.

"No," Mrs. Blessing said, pivoting slowly as she compared the names on the map with the hand-painted street signs just above the first story of each corner building. The new highlights in her brown hair sparkled as she turned the map upside down and held it high to capture the last of the light. "But this town is a maze."

We are totally lost, Birdie thought as she leaned against her suitcase. Her dad had been an awesome navigator, so neither Birdie nor her mom had ever given it much thought. They never got lost.

Until now.

"Ah, there we go. This way," her mother said, pointing to a stone archway on the far side of the square.

A rumble sounded behind them, fast and low.

Birdie dropped her suitcase handle and grabbed her mother's arm, pulling her back against one of the ancient buildings as headlights swept over them. A black car flew by, so close that their hair lifted from their shoulders in its wake.

"What the heck..." Birdie began, releasing her mom's arm and bending to retrieve her suitcase.

"It was a taxi," Mrs. Blessing said. She brushed off the front of her jeans. "I didn't think they allowed cars in these narrow lanes, but I guess they must. Are you okay?"

Birdie nodded.

"Let's get to the bed and breakfast."

They passed beneath the stone archway and found themselves on a lane so narrow Birdie thought they might be able to touch the medieval houses on either side if they stood side-by-side and spread their arms wide.

A tabby cat skittered past, banked left, and fled up a dark alley across the way.

Mrs. Blessing searched the wood and metal signs that flew like flags from the second stories of several of the homes, creaking on rusted hinges in the damp breeze.

A few blocks away a smaller bell began to toll the hour.

"There," Mrs. Blessing said, pointing to a cream-colored house a few doors down on the right-hand side. "Number 814."

As they drew closer, Birdie could make out a coat of arms on the house's swaying sign. In the center of the shield a standing bear gripped a letter B. Beneath it, black iron letters spelled out the words *t'Bruges Huis*.

Below the sign, a wooden door sat recessed from a stone landing. A numbered keypad glowed electric green on the doorframe, its modern convenience out of place against the medieval masonry.

Mrs. Blessing punched in a code, grabbed the bronze handle and pushed the door open before it could lock again.

"We made it," she whispered with a satisfied smile that reached hazel eyes that were nearly identical to Birdie's. "A few more minutes and the code would've expired."

Birdie returned her mother's smile.

They'd made it.

The first challenge had been met.

"It's late," Mrs. Blessing said, setting her luggage just inside the door. "The other guests are probably sleeping."

Birdie nodded, but she wasn't really listening.

She stepped deeper into the room.

They were in the foyer of a very old house, awash in the glow of a crystal chandelier on an automatic sensor. The soft light illuminated hundreds of tiny stone tiles on the floor, each the size of a Scrabble piece, in vibrant shades of brown, tan, and shimmering gold. The tiles were carefully arranged in ribbons of color that flowed to the center of the room, where they intertwined to form a magnificent flower.

"It's so beautiful," Birdie said.

On the left, a slender staircase hugged a mirrored wall, while closer to where they stood a blue wing-backed chair and an antique cabinet rounded out the foyer's furniture.

Beside the cabinet an archway led to a sitting room that flowed into a dining room. Mrs. Blessing pushed a small round button on the wall to light another crystal chandelier.

"Wow," she said. "The guidebook was right. This is really lovely."

"How much are we paying for this?" Birdie asked.

"Don't worry about it," her mom said, clicking off the lights.

They climbed single file to the second story of t'Bruges Huis, taking care not to bang their suitcases into the walls. Sconces lit their way, turning on one by one as they approached. They followed a carved wooden banister around a sharp corner and continued down a hallway past several closed doors, then turned again to climb the final flight of stairs to their attic room.

A handwritten note on the door read: "Welcome

Blessing Family."

Mrs. Blessing scooped the note from the door and crumpled it in her hand. She set to work twisting and jangling the skeleton key in the lock until it broke free.

To Birdie's delight, their bedroom was as lovely as the rooms downstairs.

"I can't believe you found this place," she said, staring at the dark wooden beams that sloped up the walls of the long room to form an airy peak above them. A deep casement window at the far end had been cranked open and the evening breeze swept across the warm room.

There were two single beds, one near the window and one tucked against the wall, each adorned with a pillow and a thick duvet the color of sunflowers. A writing desk with a straight-backed chair stood near a tiny closet, while a narrow door at the far end of the room led to the bathroom.

Birdie made her way to the window and knelt beside it. She crossed her arms under her chin on the broad sill.

The dark lane below was deserted. She could just make out the archway they'd passed under to the left, while to the right the cobblestones curved past the alley where the tabby cat had fled.

As Birdie watched, the tabby slinked back into the lane, stopping to scratch its long, mottled neck against the edge of a stately stone house. A moment later two tall figures emerged from the alley, their broad shoulders bent against the night.

They slowed in front of t'Bruges Huis, then disappeared beneath the overhang as they stepped up to the stone landing.

"We should get to bed," Mrs. Blessing said from across the room. "Research starts tomorrow."

Right. Her mom's research. Birdie had nearly forgotten why they were here.

"There are two men outside." She turned to face her

mother. "They're at the front door."

Mrs. Blessing shrugged. "If they're guests they'll have a code."

"But..."

"I'm sure it's fine, Birdie."

She turned back to the lane below. The men were nowhere in sight. Even the tabby had fled.

Birdie began to crank the window closed.

"Oh, leave it open," Mrs. Blessing said, heaving her suitcase onto the duvet. The bed bounced under its weight. She unzipped it and pulled out her toiletry bag. "It's quiet enough and the breeze feels good. Maybe it'll help us sleep. Come on, get changed. It's been a long day."

Birdie didn't want to argue. Besides, she was tired. She slipped into her pajamas and snuggled onto her side in the soft bed to be sure she could still see the light coming from the bathroom.

The last thing she saw as she drifted to sleep was her mother's reflection in the bathroom mirror as she wiped away the touch of make-up she'd only recently started to wear again. It was just enough to mask the dark circles beneath her eyes, circles that had appeared a year ago and stubbornly refused to leave.

Accommodations in Bruges
range from high-end, full service
hotels to cheery youth hostels.
In between are bed and breakfasts,
which many of my readers find
offer the best value for the price.

Marty McEntire's
Europe for Americans Travel Guide

CHAPTER TWO

WOO Who...

The sunlight slipped through the open window and settled on Birdie's pale yellow duvet.

WOO Who...

WOO Who...

The opening notes of a song rang out, repeating in her dream, sounding softly, again and again, impatient to be heard.

WOO Who...

As she drifted awake, Birdie was struck by the heaviness of her body in the bed.

She'd slept well. For once no nightmares climbed through her dreams.

She tried to remember the last time she'd slept so soundly.

Had it been the whole year?

WOO Who...

There it was again.

But, no, it wasn't a song. It was something else entirely.

She squinted against the morning light that swept across the attic room.

WOO Who...

woo who...

WOO Who...

She sat up slowly and peered through the open window.

The sound was definitely coming from outside, somewhere close by, amplified in the otherwise still morning.

She considered climbing from the bed to get a better view, but the breeze filtering through the window was cool on her bare arms, making the soft warmth of the duvet more inviting.

She wiggled her long toes and discovered that even her achy feet had recovered from the long walk on the uneven cobblestones the night before. She stretched her thin arms toward the ceiling, enjoying the creaky pull in her muscles. When she brought her hands back down she rubbed the sleep from her eyes.

Her mother had indeed fallen asleep, the rhythm of her breathing slow and gentle. Birdie sent up a grateful thank you. It'd been ages since she'd seen her rest so peacefully.

Rustling drew Birdie's attention back to the window.

A large gray and white dove had landed on the sill.

Its head bobbed as its wobbling glance darted from the cobblestone lane below to the bright blue sky to the warm room where Birdie lay watching.

From far away the crisp notes of the song sounded again, carried across the morning breeze.

WOO Who...

woo who...

WOO Who...

WOO WHO!

Birdie buried her head beneath the duvet as the dove's call ricocheted around the room.

"What on earth?" Mrs. Blessing murmured, her voice thick with sleep.

Birdie slipped the duvet back and peeked over it at the windowsill.

The dove continued to bob its head, oblivious to its wakeup call.

A moment later it called again, somehow even louder than before. After a beat, its partner's response traveled back to them over the breeze.

"That sounds like the beginning of a song," Mrs. Blessing said.

"That's what I thought," Birdie said, turning in the soft bed to look at her. "I was dreaming that somebody kept playing it over and over again. Then Willy showed up."

"Willy?"

"The dove," Birdie said. "I named him Willy."

"You named him?" Mrs. Blessing looked as if she might laugh but she did not. "Why? And why Willy?"

"Willy or won't he wake us up every morning?" Birdie said with a shrug.

"Oh, dear Lord I hope not," Mrs. Blessing said.

"At least we won't need to set the alarm clock."

"Well, that's looking at the bright side," her mom replied as she snuggled her head into the soft pillow. "Good to see you're getting your sense of humor back."

The words washed over Birdie like ice water.

She sat back against her pillow and rolled toward the open window.

They stayed in their beds for a while, watching Willy bob his head. Every so often he would answer another dove's call.

When it was clear neither of them were going back to sleep, Mrs. Blessing climbed from her bed, careful to avoid the wooden beams on the slanted ceiling.

"It's still pretty early," she said as she extracted a blue bathrobe from her suitcase. "According to the guidebook, breakfast starts at eight o'clock. I'm going to grab a shower."

She paused at the bathroom door.

"And Birdie?"

"Hmmm?"

"Do not let Willy fly in here."

Birdie hadn't considered that possibility.

Fortunately Willy seemed to have little interest in entering the room.

For several long minutes he listened and responded to the other dove as Birdie studied the plain-faced stone houses across the street. They rose narrow and tall to jagged points. Along each roofline, red bricks stacked like stairs marched toward the peak. Every house she'd seen in Bruges so far had some form of decorative roof like these, capping them off like wedding cakes.

Willy bobbed his head, his beady black eyes steadying enough to latch squarely on Birdie's as if to bid her farewell.

She wiggled her fingers at him.

The dove's head dipped low as if he were bowing, then he flew off in a rustle of wings and air.

"Bye, Willy."

She knew it was stupid, but she was sad to see him go.

She waited a few minutes to see if he would return. When he didn't, she slipped out of bed and stepped to the window on bare feet.

There was no sign of Willy anywhere. Even the bird that returned his call had quieted. The street below was empty, too.

She wondered what had become of the men she'd seen the night before. She hadn't heard them come in, but then she was at the very top of the house, tucked away in the attic.

She used the hand crank to push the window open a bit wider.

Several white and gray feathers lay on the outer stone sill.

Birdie checked to make sure the bathroom door was still closed, then reached out to retrieve them. They resembled quill pens, although the feathers were not as long or stiff as those used for writing.

As she pulled them into the room, the morning sun glanced off an object on the sill a few inches to the left.

Birdie leaned forward for a better look and clunked her head against the tall casement window.

"Ow."

She rubbed the pain from her forehead.

She backed up and tried again, this time cranking the window open as far as it would go. When she was sure her head and shoulders would fit, she leaned through the slender opening three stories above the quiet lane below.

The sun lighted on the object again. Its surface sparkled as if it were on fire, reflecting light back to the world.

Birdie reached to the left as far as she could.

A rogue breeze kicked up, cutting through her polka-dotted pajama top.

She shivered but pressed on.

She could barely touch it with her fingertips. It took several tries, but finally she inched it closer.

She raked the small item toward her, gasping when it flipped and nearly tumbled off the ledge. She stopped, transfixed by its brilliant sheen as it teetered half on and half off the windowsill.

She had to have it now.

Birdie leaned a precarious inch further out the window and grasped it.

Behind her, the latch on the bathroom door slid open.

Birdie pulled herself back into the room and wrapped her hand around the cool object. She used her other hand to crank the window back to its previous position then spun to face the bathroom door.

"It's almost time for breakfast," Mrs. Blessing said, coming back into the room looking refreshed. "They'll serve it in the dining room."

As if on cue, across town the heavy bell began its slow chime.

"Okay, I'll get ready," Birdie said, stepping away from the window to kneel by her suitcase. She unzipped it and retrieved a pair of jeans. As she did she slipped the small object deep into the front pocket. She quickly gathered the rest of her clothes for the day and headed for the bathroom.

"Make sure you wash your hands if you were handling those feathers," Mrs. Blessing called after her.

Birdie had forgotten about the feathers. "Right," she said.

The bathroom held a small sink, toilet, and shower stall. She hung her clothes on a hook on the back of the door, checking to make sure the object hadn't fallen out of the pocket of her jeans. She'd have to deal with that later.

She surveyed the room.

This was going to be interesting.

She considered asking her mom to come in to help her figure out the contraptions in front of her, but thought better of it. She could almost hear Jonah teasing her in the high-pitched voice he used when he mocked her, which had been often:

Mom, will you flush the toilet for me? I can't figure it out.
Mom, can you turn on the shower for me? I'm a loser.

Mom, will you wipe my butt?

She smiled weakly.

That was exactly what he would have done.

For days.

She took a deep breath and reached for the handles in the shower. If she couldn't figure out how to use the bathroom on her own then she deserved Jonah's wrath: she really was hopeless.

In the end it took several minutes longer than normal to shower and change. Every faucet and fixture she tried to use was unusual. The showerhead hung from a long hose that swiveled and shook when the water was running, threatening to flood the bathroom floor if it swung too far to the left. The water flow and temperature were controlled by strange-looking stainless steel dials instead of a simple lever. Even the toilet had a three-section push-button flusher instead of a typical handle.

After Birdie finished and pulled on her fresh outfit, she returned to the bedroom to find that her mom had straightened the beds. She was sitting at the desk with her sketchbook open.

Birdie tossed her worn pajamas and dirty clothes on top of her suitcase.

"What are you working on?" she asked.

Mrs. Blessing scratched the paper with a thin piece of charcoal. "I'm trying to remember that old farm gate we passed yesterday on the train. It wasn't medieval, but I liked the lines of it. We passed it too fast to take a picture."

"I think it was a little more curved at the top," Birdie said, studying the rough sketch over her mom's shoulder.

Mrs. Blessing adjusted the lines. "You're right. That looks closer."

She closed the book and returned the charcoal to its case. "Let's go see if breakfast is ready. I'm starved."

Breakfasts in Europe vary
from country to country.
The further north you travel,
the heartier the fare.
The farther south?
Get used to croissants
and jam.

Marty McEntire's
Europe for Americans Travel Guide

CHAPTER THREE

Birdie and Mrs. Blessing made their way down the two flights of stairs to the foyer, where the mingling aroma of bacon, eggs, toast, and coffee greeted them. A lively conversation was already in progress as they entered the sitting room.

"No, Harry, I don't think that's right," a jolly looking woman was saying. She sat at the far end of the dining room table examining a colorful map through a thin pair of reading glasses. The curtains behind her were thrown open to let in the sun and a view of a crumbling brick wall crawling with ivy.

"Oh, for Pete's sake. Let me see that map," Harry replied, his bushy white mustache wiggling as he spoke.

The woman handed it to him, shaking her head as she did. "I can't find Wijngaardstraat Street anywhere."

"It's right there, Helga," he said, smoothing the map on the fabric tablecloth and pointing to a spot on it. "Wijngaardstraat. You don't need to add street at the end: straat means street."

"Oh. Well, how am I supposed to know that?" Helga

asked.

"Marty explained it in the book."

Helga squared her ample shoulders and looked as if she were about to object but Harry spoke first.

"Oh, it doesn't matter," he said, pushing the argument away before it could begin. He tapped the map with a thick index finger. "We'll take that when we get close to the old Begijnhof. It can't be more than a fifteen minute walk from here."

"Well, look at that," Helga said, peering through her glasses to the spot where Harry was pointing. "It's right there."

She winked at the lanky boy sitting across from her and then removed her glasses, folding them carefully and setting them beside her plate. "Maybe it's time for a new pair."

The boy managed a smile that looked crooked on his angular face. Birdie thought he seemed infinitely relieved when a tall, sturdy woman bustled through a sliding pocket door holding a plate that steamed with thick slices of bacon.

Mrs. Blessing pushed Birdie gently toward the dining room.

"Well, good morning," the woman said, noticing the newcomers at once. "You must be the Blessings."

Her words were touched with a Dutch accent and she wore her thick blond and white hair pulled back in a chignon at the nape of her neck. Her face lit with a bright smile.

She gestured to two empty seats with the plate of bacon. "Come, sit, sit. Welcome to t'Bruges Huis. I'm Mrs. Devon. Would you like some coffee? Juice?"

"Coffee would be wonderful," Mrs. Blessing said. "Thank you."

"And you?" she asked Birdie as she scooped several slices of bacon onto the boy's plate. "Orange juice, I think?"

"Yes, thank you," Birdie replied as her stomach

rumbled.

Mrs. Devon hustled back through the door, which slid closed behind her. Before it did Birdie caught a glimpse of a sunny kitchen beyond.

"Good morning," Helga said with a smile. "I'm Helga Hinnershitz and this is my husband, Harry. We're from Ohio. Akron."

"It's nice to meet you," Mrs. Blessing said. "I'm Maria Blessing and this is my daughter, Birdie. We're from a small town in Pennsylvania called Bamburg."

"Oh, sure. I've heard of Bamburg," Mr. Hinnershitz said. His voice had a booming quality that filled the room. "There's a state university there, isn't there?"

"Yes, that's right," Mrs. Blessing said.

"And what brings you to the fine city of Bruges?" he asked.

Birdie's heart quickened but her mother didn't miss a beat.

"I'm a designer," she said, trying on her new title. Birdie had to admit it sounded good. "Birdie and I are exploring Europe this summer to get ideas for a new line of clothing and home accessories I'm working on. It has a medieval theme."

"Well isn't that fascinating," Mrs. Hinnershitz said, leaning forward on her generous elbows. "And a wonderful excuse to see the old world."

Birdie stole a glance at the silent boy sitting next to her as the women continued talking. He was much taller than she was, and much taller than Jonah had been, but she thought he was about her age.

He was clearly hungry: He was eating like this was his first and last meal.

He caught her looking at him and smiled awkwardly through a mouthful of bacon.

Birdie looked down at her empty plate, her cheeks

growing warm. Now it was her turn to be relieved when Mrs. Devon returned with their drinks.

"Have you met Ben?" she asked, setting a bright orange glass of fresh-squeezed juice on Birdie's placemat. "He's visiting Bruges with his uncle. Will Mr. Martin be joining us this morning?"

Ben finished chewing and swallowed another large bite before responding. "I'm afraid not. He's still upstairs, ma'am."

His voice was a bit deeper than Birdie expected, and rich with a slow drawl.

"He was fixing to get some work done this morning," he continued. "I was hungry so I came down without him."

"Yes, the young men are always hungry," Mrs. Devon said cheerfully.

A memory of Jonah sitting on the back patio devouring an ear of corn-on-the-cobb slipped across Birdie's consciousness. She pushed it away.

She thought she saw a shadow cross her mother's face, too.

Keep it together, Mom, she thought.

"I've seen many young men at this table, and always they are hungry, yes?"

Ben nodded his agreement.

"How long have you been running the bed and breakfast?" Mrs. Hinnershitz asked.

"Oh, about thirty years now."

"Well it's just lovely," she said.

"Thank you."

Mrs. Devon offered Birdie and Mrs. Blessing several choices for breakfast, and they opted to share an omelet, toast and bacon. Mrs. Devon nodded appreciatively and slipped back into the kitchen to prepare it.

"We found this place in the *Europe for Americans Travel Guide*," Mrs. Hinnershitz said after the kitchen door slid closed. "Have you heard of it? It's the best guidebook I've ever read. The author, Marty McEntire, is full of great tips and he is so funny, too." She pulled the book from a large bag hanging on the back of her chair.

Birdie recognized the green and yellow cover at once.

Mrs. Blessing nodded approvingly. "Marty McEntire helped me plan this whole trip. That book's been like my bible."

"My uncle has that book," Ben said. "He has another one, too, that's a guide to every brewery and bar in eleven countries."

Birdie raised her eyebrows at him.

He raised his back at her. They were dark and a little bushy, setting off the deep brown eyes beneath them. His hair was nearly black and reminded Birdie of an untamed mop.

Mrs. Hinnershitz continued, "Yes, we met Ben's uncle, Noah Martin, yesterday morning at breakfast. He's a brewmaster. They're from Texas. Austin, right, Ben?"

Ben broke his stare with Birdie.

"Not exactly, ma'am. I'm from Marshall Falls, but Uncle Noah's from Austin. He's not a brewmaster yet, but he sure does want to be."

"Oh yes, that's right, that's right," Mrs. Hinnershitz said. "Our granddaughter is here, too." She eyed the sitting room expectantly.

Birdie followed her gaze but there was no one there.

"Not up yet," Mr. Hinnershitz grumbled, not hiding his disapproval.

"No, I suppose not," Mrs. Hinnershitz said. She paused, sizing up Birdie and Ben with her cheerful blue eyes. "You can meet our granddaughter, Kayla, later. She's about your age, I think. She's seventeen."

"Oh, I'm fifteen," Birdie said.

"Fifteen, ma'am," Ben said with a nod.

"Well, she's older then," Mrs. Hinnershitz said, not bothering to hide a sigh.

The pocket door slid open and Mrs. Devon returned with the Blessings' breakfast.

"Here you go," she said as she set the plates on the mats. "And what about you, young man? Would you like anything else from the kitchen?"

"No thank you, ma'am, I'm good," he said, reaching for a raspberry pastry on the top tier of a serving rack. It stood where a floral centerpiece had been the night before.

"Well, are you about done, Helga?" Mr. Hinnershitz asked, pushing his chair away from the table. He looked entirely too big for the small piece of furniture.

Mrs. Hinnershitz wiped her mouth with the cloth napkin that had been covering her lap. "I am. Do you think we should wake Kayla for breakfast?"

Mr. Hinnershitz frowned and the edges of his white mustache descended like a curtain around his lips. "I think we should have woken her up two hours ago."

"Well, too late now," Mrs. Hinnershitz said. "No use getting upset about it."

She turned to the Blessings. "It was a pleasure to meet you both. Enjoy your time exploring Bruges today. You're going to love it. We've been here three days and we could stay a dozen more."

"Thank you. You too," Mrs. Blessing said.

The Hinnershitzes collected their things, bid farewell to Ben and Mrs. Devon, and made their way out of the room. Birdie listened to their heavy steps slow as they climbed the creaking stairs.

She dug into her breakfast, which tasted as delicious as it had smelled. She tried to remember the last time she'd had a hot breakfast and drew a blank. At home she grabbed some cereal or yogurt from a largely empty fridge, if she bothered to eat at all.

"What are we going to do today?" she asked when she had taken the last bite of toast. "You said last night that research starts today."

"Well," Mrs. Blessing said, glancing at the sunshine pooling on the sitting room floor, "I thought we'd rent bikes and explore the town that way. There's a rental shop a couple of blocks away. When you're done with breakfast we can get ready and go."

"I'm done," Birdie said, wiping her hands and placing the napkin on the table.

"Okay, great. I'll just run up to the room to get my things and then we can leave," Mrs. Blessing said. "Do you need anything?"

"Nope, I'm good. I brought my daypack down earlier. I'll just wait in the foyer."

"Okay." Mrs. Blessing leaned across Birdie. "Bye, Ben."

Ben nodded farewell and reached for another pastry.

"Bye, Birdie," he said with a grin.

The Basilica of the Holy Blood houses
Bruges's most famous relic, a flask said
to contain a drop of the blood of Jesus. The
Count of Flanders sent it to Bruges sometime
in the thirteenth century, along with other items
looted from Constantinople during the crusades.
You'll find relics - drops of blood, fragments of bone,
sometimes whole skeletons - sprinkled at churches
all across Europe. The most influential
churches generally received
the most coveted relics.

Marty McEntire's
Europe for Americans Travel Guide

CHAPTER FOUR

Birdie settled on the second-to-last step in the mirrored foyer, her chin tucked into her hand as she leaned forward, elbows on her knees. The patchwork daypack holding her sketchbook, pencils, camera, and jacket sat beside her. She wished she had her phone, but her mother hadn't let her bring it.

"Who are you planning to call?" her mom had asked.

"No one," she said. "But I'd like to be able to take pictures."

"Bring a camera."

That had been the end of the conversation and she hadn't seen her phone since. She assumed it was packed up with everything else in the storage unit at home. She could have fought to bring it, and her mom may have given in, but there really was no one to call, no one to text, no one to communicate with at all. And Lord knew no one would be sending her a message.

She tried to forget about her phone and the mess she now called her life. If there was one good thing about spending the summer in Europe with her mother, it was that she could escape for a little while. No one knew her here. No one knew the story. She could be anyone.

Maybe even someone normal.

She stared absently at the mosaic tiles that coalesced into the flower on the floor. A few of the pieces had chipped over time or were missing altogether, but she could tell that each tiny tile had been precisely laid into a flowing pattern to create ribbons of golds, tans, and browns. One ribbon of deep red punctuated them all. She tracked it to the center of the bloom, where it exploded into different shades.

As she visually followed the sweep of a brown ribbon of tiles, Birdie remembered the sparkling object she'd picked up from the windowsill that morning. It had slipped her mind at breakfast. Now she half stood, dug into the pocket of her jeans to retrieve it, and settled back down on the step.

She turned the cool piece over in her palm.

It reminded her of a smooth river stone, yet not exactly. It was about the size of a quarter, only more oblong than round. It appeared as dark as cinnamon at first, but a closer inspection revealed a golden sheen that spread like glowing sand across it.

Birdie rubbed the glasslike surface with her thumb, enjoying the cool feel of it against her warm skin. As she rubbed, the golden speckles shimmered brightly and began to swim. It seemed to grow warmer, too.

"Whatcha got there?" Ben asked as he came out of the sitting room. His long face and crooked smile marked him as harmless despite his towering size. Now that he was standing, Birdie could see that he wore tan cargo shorts and a black t-shirt with a flaming guitar on the front.

"I'm not sure," Birdie said, opening her hand wider. "I found it on the windowsill this morning."

She turned it over on her palm and showed it to him.

Her breath caught.

The gold speckles weren't just shimmering on this side,

they were flowing and undulating toward the center, creating rivers of golden light.

"Whoa, that's awesome," Ben said, taking a knee beside her to get a better look. As they watched, the rivers collided and formed a glistening, multi-petaled flower, just like the one on the floor at her feet, only all in gold. It was stunning, like a brilliant jewel set in a copper pool.

"It's the flower that's on this floor," she said.

Ben looked at the tiny tiles under his long black skateboarding sneakers. "You know, I think you're right."

"It's hot, too," Birdie said, shifting it into her other hand. "Feel it."

She dropped it onto his palm.

"Holy crow," he said. "You're not kidding." He studied the golden flower. "You said you found this on the windowsill?"

Birdie nodded.

"That's crazy. Where do you think it came from?"

"I have no idea."

"Maybe the last people who stayed in your room left it there." He turned it over in his palm as a slow smile spread across his face. "Stinks to be them. This thing is pretty freaking cool."

"Are you two looking forward to your day exploring Bruges?" Mrs. Devon asked, startling them both. They'd been concentrating so hard that they hadn't heard her come into the foyer.

"Oh, um, yes I am," Birdie replied, as Ben dropped the small stone back onto her palm. She instinctively wrapped her fingers around it, shielding it from sight. Its heat radiated into her hand.

"Yes, me too," Ben said, getting back to his feet. "Uncle Noah and I are going to tour the brewery."

"You'll probably see aventurine in the brewery gift shop," Mrs. Devon said, nodding toward Birdie's closed hand. "There's a legend about it, something about the shifting sands of time. They say it was quite rare, a special glass that could be made only in Venice."

"Aventurine?" Birdie asked.

"Yes. That's right. That's what that stone in your hand is called. Aventurine. It's not stone, though, it's glass. Well, the one in your hand is made to look like glass. True aventurine was so beautiful that everyone believed it was a gemstone. I don't remember the whole story, but it was once highly coveted. Pilgrims would spend their whole lives searching for a piece of it."

"Pilgrims?" Birdie asked.

"Oh, yes, well, right. You have studied United States history at school? So I can see why you might be confused by the word pilgrims," Mrs. Devon said, leaning against the dark cabinet. "There were pilgrims long before the ones who crossed the Atlantic Ocean in search of religious freedom in the new world. There are still pilgrims today, in fact. A pilgrim is someone who goes on a pilgrimage."

Birdie opened her palm and shifted the aventurine to her other hand. It was still warm, but not as hot as it had been. She studied it while Mrs. Devon continued. Even with its dark color it was translucent like glass. The gold speckles had floated within the opaque space as they formed the flower.

"A pilgrimage is a journey, usually a very long journey, for a purpose that is significant to a person's spiritual beliefs or religion. So the pilgrims who went to America were on a journey to find a place where they could freely practice their religion, which was a different religion than the one that was accepted in England at the time. Other pilgrims will walk from country to country to visit important cathedrals or temples as a way of showing their devotion to God. Some pilgrims come to Bruges even now to visit our Basilica of the Holy Blood."

"What about the glass?" Ben asked.

"Well, that was a symbol of an earlier belief system that was based on magic and mysticism. In the very early Middle Ages, before Christianity took hold across Europe, people would spend their whole lives searching for that special piece of glass."

"And now they sell it at the brewery?" Ben asked as the ringing of church bells drifted through the open sitting room windows.

"Well, yes," Mrs. Devon said with a chuckle. "They are not the real Venetian glass. They are toys that go along with the legend. Souvenirs for the tourists, really. I don't know anyone who lives in Bruges who has one."

"Oh," Birdie said, gently running her fingers over its smooth surface. The flower held tight. It didn't seem like a toy to her, at least not the kind she'd ever played with before. "They must be expensive."

"Well, no, not really. I don't think they are expensive at all," Mrs. Devon said, smiling at Birdie. She stood up straighter and wiped her hands on a kitchen towel she'd been holding. As she did, Birdie noticed a stocky young man in a hat and long coat push the door open at the far end of the hall.

It must be cooler out than she thought.

The man knelt down and ran a large, dirty hand over the tiles on the floor near the door and then pulled a small tool from his ill-fitting coat. He began prying up one of the miniature tiles.

Ben and Birdie exchanged curious glances, but Mrs. Devon didn't seem at all bothered by his appearance.

Upstairs a door slammed shut, as if caught by a breeze.

"Are you sure you have everything you need, Birdie?" Mrs. Blessing called as she turned the corner at the top of the landing and made her way down the final flight of stairs behind them.

Birdie stood to let her pass. "I think so."

She pulled her blue jacket from her daypack and slipped it on, then put the piece of glass into the pocket.

"And where are you headed today?" Mrs. Devon asked.

"We're going to rent bikes and explore the town," Mrs. Blessing said.

"Oh, it's a beautiful day for it," Mrs. Devon replied. "There is a chance of storms this afternoon but otherwise it should be cool and sunny."

"I just need to find the bike shop," Mrs. Blessing said. "Can you point me in the right direction on this map?"

She unfolded her map on the cabinet and outlined the route she thought they should take.

As the women studied the map, Ben caught Birdie's eye and nodded toward the door at the end of the hall.

"Where did he go?" Birdie mouthed.

Ben shrugged.

"Yes, yes, that's perfect," Mrs. Devon said, nodding approvingly. "Just keep your eyes open for this turn." She pointed to an intersection on the map. "It's barely an alleyway. That's where most people lose their way."

The rumble of feet sounded above them and they took a collective step away from the bottom of the stairs.

A man in his late thirties with shaggy brown hair and dark eyes appeared on the landing. Like Ben, he wore a pair of long cargo shorts and a black t-shirt.

"Oh, morning, then," he said, slowing his descent when he realized there were other people there. "You about ready, Ben?" he asked.

"Yes sir," Ben replied.

Birdie looked from one to the other. Their resemblance was striking. They were both tall with hair that was just a bit too long to be respectable, although Ben's was a shade darker. Even their dark brown eyes caught the light in a similar way. If she hadn't already heard that this was Ben's uncle, she would have guessed they were brothers.

"Ben tells me you're off to our brewery today," Mrs. Devon said in the same pleasant tone she'd used with Mrs. Blessing.

"Yes, ma'am, and we need to get a move on if we're going to make the first tour."

Ben took a step toward the front door.

"No breakfast, then?" Mrs. Devon asked.

"Uh, no ma'am, not today, thank you though," Uncle Noah said. "Ben, did you eat?"

He nodded.

"Okay, let's go then." Uncle Noah tipped his shaggy head at the rest of them and pulled the door open. A moment later he and Ben were gone.

Perhaps the best way to explore Bruges
is by getting lost deep in its streets and parks
on a bicycle, away from the tour bus groups
that overrun the Market Square.
Save your shopping for later in the day,
when the crowds thin and the
stylish clothing and shoe stores beckon.
Be sure to indulge in the plentiful
samples at the chocolate shops, too.
No trip to Belgium is complete
without chocolate.

Marty McEntire's
Europe for Americans Travel Guide

CHAPTER FIVE

The cobbled lanes and passageways that had been deserted the night before were now thick with well-dressed locals and sneakered tourists, some enjoying baked goods and coffee at sidewalk cafés, others gazing at lace dresses and leather shoes artfully arranged in shop windows. A curious aroma of sugary sweets and sea air swelled, as if conspiring to lure them deeper into the maze.

Birdie and Mrs. Blessing passed from sun to shade as they followed the twisting lanes to a mid-sized square. It was alive with people snapping photos of a Gothic building whose triple spires loomed like needles against the blue sky. Its soaring windows were offset by dozens of stone statues adorning the facade.

"Let's see," Mrs. Blessing said, stopping to turn her map upside down and then righting it again. "This must be Burg Square. Yes, there's the Basilica of the Holy Blood on the corner. And that building," she glanced up from the map at the imposing structure, "is the Town Hall, believe it or not. Do you see the flags between the spires?"

A drumbeat cut through the calm morning air, drawing

Birdie's attention away from the ornate buildings and toward an ancient archway tucked under the left side of the Town Hall. Tourists passed beneath it in a steady stream, forming a rolling bottleneck as they dug for their phones and cameras.

The beat grew heavier, vibrating against the stone archway and exploding into an electronic bass as a half-dozen teenage boys wove through the tourists and entered the square.

Birdie glanced at her mom, who shrugged.

The boys were similarly dressed in shorts that fell just above their knees, collared shirts, and low-slung leather sneakers. They carried deflated backpacks and their hair, in varying shades of blond and light brown, was respectably cropped. The last in line balanced a silver boom box on his shoulder.

The boys kept pace with the music, holding their heads high and avoiding eye contact as they crossed the square. Birdie felt the vibration in the soles of her shoes as they skirted her, then listened to the music fade as they disappeared down one of the cobblestone lanes.

She found herself wondering what Ben would have thought of them.

"Guess they live here," Mrs. Blessing said as the beat was replaced by the tolling of a bell.

"I guess."

She considered the groups of people clogging the square.

"It would be weird to live in a place like this wouldn't it?"

"Weird?" Her mother had retrieved a camera from her daypack and was lining up a picture of the Town Hall.

"Well, all these strangers here all the time, dropping in, taking pictures of your town, and then leaving."

"Not before spending their money. Don't forget that," Mrs. Blessing said, returning the camera to her bag. "Just look at the line at the waffle stand." She gestured toward a pocket park at the edge of the square and began walking toward it. "Bruges has been in the business of welcoming strangers for centuries."

"Yeah, I guess," Birdie said, falling into step beside her. "I still think it'd be weird."

"Speaking of weird, don't you think the bed and breakfast is an odd choice for Ben and his uncle?"

"What do you mean?" Birdie paused to study a bronze statue of two masked dancers at the entrance to the park. Their graceful forms intertwined as they reached toward the sky. They were lovely and sad at the same time, so beautiful yet marred and perforated by decades of exposure to rain and air.

"Well, it's, I don't know, kind of feminine I guess."

Birdie shrugged. "Mr. Hinnershitz is staying there."

"Yes, but he's with Mrs. Hinnershitz."

"I don't know, Mom. They need to stay somewhere." Birdie pulled her camera from her daypack and snapped a photo of the statue. "And Ben did say his uncle has the same guidebook that you do."

"Yes, that's true," Mrs. Blessing said, stepping to the side as a woman on a bicycle passed them. "Come on, let's get those bikes."

"Mom?" Birdie called a few hours later as they bumped across the cobblestones. She stole a glance at the dark clouds making their way swiftly across the blue sky.

"I know, Birdie," Mrs. Blessing replied as she steered her bike into a tight alley.

Thunder rumbled overhead as a breeze whipped between the buildings, pushing them into a courtyard thick with people huddled around tables and eyeing the sky nervously. A red brick building enclosed the courtyard on three sides.

Mrs. Blessing pointed to a bike rack under a canopy near a door.

"There," she said. "Quickly!"

They dismounted and walked their bikes through the crowd as the first fat drops of rain began to fall.

Mrs. Blessing twisted the keys to lock the bikes as Birdie grabbed their daypacks from the front baskets. They sprinted up the brick stairs and inside the building just as the sky opened up.

"Whew!" Mrs. Blessing said, fluffing the raindrops from her hair. "We made it."

"Yes, but where are we?" Birdie asked, squeezing into an open space between a white-haired man in golf shorts and a family from China. She rubbed the raindrops from her bare arms and shivered. She pulled the jacket from her daypack and slipped it back on.

"Well," Mrs. Blessing said, taking a place beside Birdie as rain pounded against the outside of the building. "I guess we're at the brewery."

Thunder clapped outside.

"Want to take a tour?" Mrs. Blessing leaned in close so Birdie could hear her.

"Why not?" Birdie shrugged. "It's better than getting soaked."

"There might be some cool old designs inside, who knows," Mrs. Blessing said, rummaging in her daypack for her wallet.

Birdie thought that was likely. Although the merchandise in the shop was new, the building looked like it had been around for ages.

"I'll get the tickets," she said.

"Okay," Birdie replied. "I'm going to check out the gift shop."

While her mom jostled through the crowd and got in line behind a young couple to buy the tickets, Birdie scouted the gift shop for aventurine. She wanted to see if Mrs. Devon was right when she told Ben that they sold the pieces of glass here, and if she was, how much they cost.

She passed a round t-shirt rack, and skirted an even larger sweatshirt rack, then passed by a crate of beer bottles whose black labels had jeering yellow and purple jesters on the front.

The copper-colored stones sat in a bin along the wall near the back door, next to a half dozen other bins filled with trinkets. One held miniature Dutch windmills; another held what looked like small pipe organs. Birdie paused and picked one up. It said *carillon* on the back next to a tiny metal handle.

She twisted the handle and a hollow, mechanical song played, briefly attracting the attention of the other patrons in the gift shop, who quickly lost interest when they saw Birdie standing with the toy.

"Hey, Birdie."

Birdie looked up, surprised to see Ben come up beside her. "Hi Ben. Wait. You're still here?"

She clicked the handle back into place and the music stopped. She set the toy back in its bin.

He smiled. "Oh, yeah. We're still here. Don't think we'll be leaving anytime soon, either."

"Where's your uncle?"

Ben motioned to the ticket line.

"You haven't gone on a tour yet? What have you been doing?"

"Oh, we've been on the tour. But Uncle Noah has more questions so we're going again."

"We're going on the next one, too."

"Cool. It's not so bad. You'll learn a lot about beer, anyway. Hey, did you see the bin of toys Mrs. Devon told us about? It's right down here."

They passed a few other bins that contained bottle

openers of several shapes and sizes, and key chains made from rubber medallions the size of chocolate chip cookies, all with the unsettling jester smiling out at them.

What interested Birdie, however, was the bin that overflowed with stones that looked like the aventurine nestled safely in her jacket pocket.

Above the bin a sign read *Magisch Venetiaans Aventurine* in gold lettering.

Below the name, in tiny print, the legend unfurled, first in Dutch, then with the English translation underneath:

> *In the early days of Bruges, when its seaport served as a major center of trade and commerce, goods from all over the world flowed through town on their way to destinations throughout Europe. English, French and Dutch mingled as the languages of business. Mysterious sailors from distant lands brought spices, silks, and amazing inventions to sell on the Markt.*
>
> *One such sailor arrived after a harrowing journey from Venice bearing dozens of miniature boxes made of rare wood. The ornate boxes created such a sensation with their blue and gold marbling that eager buyers bought them in less than a day. Soon, every wealthy home in Bruges had a box on its mantelpiece.*
>
> *According to the legend, a well-respected lace merchant discovered three oval jewels in a hidden compartment in the bottom of his box. When he examined them, he found that they were quite unusual: Golden sparkles swirled when they were rubbed, forming simple shapes. The merchant soon realized the jewels were made of a mysterious Venetian glass called aventurine, and that each shape that formed opened a window to the past.*
>
> *As word spread of the magical glass, people came from far and wide to catch a glimpse of days gone by.*

*The man was open at first, even employing his children
to help the seekers. But others were not so kind, and
accused him of unleashing the plague from the past as
people began to fall ill. His box and the aventurine
were taken to the Basilica of the Holy Blood, never to
be seen again. The merchant and his family fled Bruges
in the night. No one knows what became of them.*

Birdie finished reading the legend and glanced around
the brightly lit gift shop. The crowd had swelled in
anticipation of another tour.

"So it's just a toy about an old legend that got some poor
dude run out of town," Ben said as he finished reading the
passage. "And it costs a whole whopping euro."

He picked up a piece of aventurine from the bin and
turned it over in his hand. He rubbed a round section on
the back and a door materialized out of gold flake.

He raised his eyebrows. "It's different than the one in
your pocket."

Something looked off to Birdie, too, as she watched Ben
rub the toy.

She reached down and picked one up from the bin.

It wasn't a piece of glass at all. It was made of hard
rubber like the key chains. The place where the gold flake
formed a picture was a bubble sticker with gold sparkles
inside.

"Oh," Birdie breathed.

"What?" Ben asked, tossing the toy back into the bin. It
bounced around as it hit the others, then settled against its
twins.

"You're right. It's not the same," Birdie said. "The piece
of glass I found. It's not like these. It's not a toy."

"Maybe yours was from one of the expensive gift shops
on the Markt."

"The glass is completely different."

"English Tour!" a woman called from the front of the store. "English Tour begins now!"

"Ben?"

They turned to see Uncle Noah crossing the gift shop. He towered over the other patrons. "Time to go."

For a moment it looked like Ben was going to ignore his uncle, but then he relented.

"See you later, Birdie," he said.

"Yeah, okay," she replied. "See you later."

She watched them gather with the rest of the crowd near a door that led to a tasting room. Her mom was there, too, and she motioned for Birdie to join her. She took one last look at the toys in the bins and then maneuvered through the shop to join the others.

Belgium is world renowned for its beer, and the quirky brewery in Bruges lives up to the hype. Try to catch the first or last tour of the day to avoid the rush. Each tour ends with a free glass of their signature brew.

Marty McEntire's
Europe for Americans Travel Guide

CHAPTER SIX

"Usually we begin in the courtyard," the tour guide said pleasantly from under the broad covered porch where they had all been ushered, "but not today, okay?"

She gestured to the rain, which was coating the now-deserted tables and chairs. Half-full glasses of beer stood abandoned as the wind whipped the decorative umbrellas meant to protect them.

"Good idea," Uncle Noah said from behind them. He was standing with Ben on the far end of the porch. Ben noticed Birdie look over and lifted two fingers in a wave. She nodded to him and then turned back to the guide.

"*Hallo*, yes, welcome. Good afternoon," the tour guide said as the group arranged itself in an arc around her. She was shorter than any of the people on the tour, and sported a delighted smile, a pixie haircut, and close-set brown eyes that twinkled with mischief as she spoke.

"My name is Elsa. I speak English, yes? But it is not my first language so I make mistakes, okay? Already I am sorry if I make any."

"Your English sounds great to me," Ben offered.

"Oh, yes, thank you very much," the tour guide replied, her cheeks going pink.

"So, yes. I am Elsa and we will spend the next, oh, hour or so together in the brewery. We will go up," she pointed toward the top of the building, "up many stairs, okay? But you will see the new and the old and learn how we make the famous Belgian beer."

The brewery, Elsa told them, was first mentioned in the town's historical documents in the 1500s. Although it had changed hands over time, the current brewmasters still used some of the same recipes that had been perfected over many centuries to ensure they were brewing the best quality beer.

They followed Elsa into the brewery through a wide steel door at the far end of the porch and into a strikingly modern room that was bright and clean with drains in the floor. It was at architectural odds with the wooden porch and crumbling red brick they'd seen outside.

The sterile room was illuminated by fluorescent lights and filled with enormous stainless steel tanks. The air smelled of homemade bread and apple cider vinegar.

"This is our newest section of the brewery," Elsa began. "As you can see, it has the most modern equipment for making beer. We make batches here, and then send them through a wonderful underground pipeline to a factory outside of the city. The beer gets bottled there. The beer we make here at the original brewery is also consumed in our tasting room, which you will see later," she smiled knowingly to the group. "Our visitors also buy it in bottles from our gift shop, which you will see also again before you leave."

She took a moment to explain the types of storage tanks in the room and then said, "Any questions before we move on?"

"What is that?" Ben asked. The group had rearranged itself as it entered the room and he was now towering above the people next to him just a few feet behind Birdie. He pointed to a foot-tall silver statue perched in an alcove near the ceiling. It seemed very old and looked out of place in the modern room.

"Oh," Elsa said smiling broadly at Ben. "That is our dear St. Arnold, the patron saint of beer. He saved Bruges by making everyone drink beer."

The group chuckled.

"Yes. It is true," Elsa said, shaking her pixie as if she could barely believe it herself. "St. Arnold was a monk who came to Bruges during an outbreak of plague. Plague, as you know, was a terrible sickness that caused your skin to erupt in great oozing boils and then you died."

Elsa made a face to show just how disgusting this was, then she continued, "Yes, very fast people died. It was spread through water contaminated by rats and there were no antibiotics to treat it. More than two-thirds of the population of Europe died, which was why the plague was called the Black Death.

"When he came to town to treat the suffering," Elsa continued, "St. Arnold noticed that none of the men who worked at the brewery were sick. Then he realized that the workers drank beer with their meals instead of water because," she paused as she shrugged and threw her hands in the air, "they were lazy?"

Everyone laughed.

"Or maybe they were just tired," she said. "You see, they had to walk all the way to the pump in the center of town if they wanted water, but the beer was right here. So St. Arnold ordered everyone in town to start drinking beer, saving many, many lives, you see."

"Why did that work?" asked the young woman who had been in front of Birdie's mom in the ticket line. Her accent was Spanish but her English was perfect.

"Oh, yes, well, to make beer is a similar process to

making tea, except you steep grains in boiling water rather than tea leaves. Boiling killed the plague bacteria that lurked in the water, making the beer safe to drink. So you see, our dear St. Arnold saved Bruges."

"Did the workers walk around drunk all the time?" Ben asked.

"Well, some, maybe, who knows?" Elsa wobbled in her heavy-duty black work shoes as if she'd had a few too many, and then continued in good humor. "But most people didn't. They'd drink one glass of beer with breakfast, one with lunch and one with dinner, but it was a very mild beer without much alcohol in it at all. You couldn't do that now with the higher potency brews."

"Definitely not," Uncle Noah agreed wholeheartedly from his place beside Ben.

"Yes, he knows," Elsa laughed again. "Any other questions before we move on?"

Hearing none, Elsa led them through a door at the far end of the room.

The glare of the modern fluorescent lights was replaced with natural sunlight from towering windows at each end of a broad hallway. In the far corner, a spiral staircase crafted from raised metal grates curled up a red brick tower and out of sight.

At Elsa's direction, the group climbed the dimly lit tower in a single-file line, spiraling up several stories until a narrow sliver of light appeared. They stepped out onto a catwalk made of an open metal grate. Birdie peered between her sneakers to see what had to be a three-story drop beneath their suspended bridge.

"Watch your step," Mrs. Blessing said as if she were a child, taking Birdie's hand in hers and patting it as they walked across the catwalk, which swayed lightly from the weight of the tour group. A door at the end led to a long room lined with red bricks. Old-fashioned brewing equipment stood in each corner and yellowing photographs hung in simple wooden frames on the exposed walls.

As Elsa continued her explanation, Birdie put her hands in her jacket pockets. The aventurine was there, warm and smooth against her skin. She rubbed her thumb over it as she examined the black-and-white photos. They showed unsmiling men dressed in heavy coats and broad-brimmed hats with kegs of beer stacked nearby.

Next to her, Mrs. Blessing considered the centuries' old markings in the thick beams above their heads.

"And here," Elsa said, "is a door to nowhere."

Steamy sunlight flooded the room as she slid open a massive wooden door that led to nothing except a steep drop to the ground several stories below.

"This was where the workmen loaded in the grains," Elsa explained. "They used hoists to drag the heavy bags up from the waiting wagons below."

Ben stepped close to the edge of the doorframe.

"Quite a drop," he said, teetering momentarily before Elsa silently guided him back to the group. He merged in next to his uncle and offered up that funny crooked smile.

Uncle Noah did not smile back.

The tour continued up a second spiral staircase. Birdie stepped into the darkened tower behind Ben. He stooped as he climbed, but his head still grazed the red brick walls.

Birdie climbed through the dim space, her sneakers barely fitting on the angled rungs even when she turned her feet to climb the stairs sideways. She stayed back far enough to ensure that she wouldn't get knocked in the teeth if one of Ben's sneakers slipped.

She climbed for what felt like a long time unsure where she was headed. As she neared the top, each curve of the stairs became increasingly brighter until she emerged into the open air.

"Hey, Birdie," Ben said, shielding his eyes from the sun as he moved away from the stairwell. "Check this out."

Birdie squinted, giving her eyes time to adjust to the brightness. When she opened them fully, she realized that they were no longer in the building at all, but on a broad, flat roof. The clouds had parted and the rainwater at her feet steamed from the heat of the sun.

Mrs. Blessing climbed up from the stairwell and made a beeline for a weathered copper rainspout formed into the shape of a gargoyle, rummaging in her daypack for a camera as she went.

Birdie wandered to the other side of the open space. The orange-red gabled roofs of the town's many houses spread out in all directions. She pulled her camera from her daypack, too.

"Looks cool from up here, doesn't it?" Ben asked, making his way over to stand beside her.

Birdie nodded.

All below her a colorful carpet tumbled forward, decorated with ribbons of sparkling canals that wove through the scenery like country lanes. Long narrow boats packed with tourists pushed slowly through the waters, following a loop that took them close to the town's back doors. Brightly colored pansies and petunias erupted from window boxes that hung in the eves of even the most modest houses. Modern windmills turned lazily in the distance.

"It doesn't look anything like where I live in Texas," Ben said, following Birdie's gaze across the rooftops. "It's like a completely different world."

From this angle she could easily see the church steeples and bell towers that rose up all over town, serving as constant guideposts in the confusion of the streets. People moved like mice far below, the crowd thickening as it neared the Markt.

"Look at all of the people down there," Birdie said.

"They have no idea that if they just walked a couple of blocks that way," she pointed toward a quiet curve of lane, "they'd have the whole town to themselves."

"They're in a hurry, that's all," Ben said. "You know, checking off the must-do list in their Marty McEntire books."

Birdie laughed. "I guess. I can't talk, though. We were down there earlier, too, eating Marty's recommended fries."

"Oh, *des frites*," Ben said, adopting a French accent. "*Magnifique!*"

"They were pretty good."

"They're awesome," Ben said. "Best lunch yet. Did you go for the classic Belgian version with mayonnaise?"

Birdie shook her head. "I stuck with plain and tried a little curry ketchup."

"Yeah, I went for the ones with beef gravy."

They watched the world below for a while.

"So that piece of glass you found is pretty wild," Ben said, turning to face her.

Birdie pulled the aventurine from her jacket pocket and held it up. The sun sparkled off its surface.

"You'd better put it away," he said. "Wouldn't want to drop it into the canal."

"No," Birdie said, turning it over in her palm before putting it back into her pocket. "But you're right. It is pretty wild. What do you think made the gold sparkles move around like that?"

Ben thought for a minute. "Not sure. Maybe some kind of magnetism?"

"That would mean it wasn't really gold."

Ben shrugged. "Got me."

An older woman pushed past them, trailing her grandson. She caught him around the middle then lifted him into her arms as he squirmed to get away.

"Everything is so old and packed together like a maze,"

Birdie said. "It just makes me want to explore it all. Let's check it out from over there."

Their sneakers squeaked as they moved across the wet rubber to the other end of the roof, angling their way through the equally awed tourists to a spot near the edge. A single handrail encircled them, although it looked as if it were more for show than for keeping anyone from tumbling down to the alley far below.

Ben walked up and grabbed the railing, leaning over it at the waist.

Birdie suppressed an urge to grab his arm and pull him back. She stayed a few inches from the railing to be safe, and then considered the view from this side.

She followed the sweep of a canal to a tranquil park with benches, well-manicured flowerbeds, and ancient trees. A few people strolled there as swans and ducks floated on the water. A towering iron gate on the far end of the park opened into a courtyard filled with windswept trees that cast shade across an overgrown lawn. A circle of simple white bungalows and a faded brick church sat within the tall stone walls.

"The canals are cool," Ben said. "Have you done the cruise yet?"

"Not yet. It's on my mom's list."

"We did it yesterday. I talked Uncle Noah into it after the Hinnershitzes mentioned it at breakfast."

"Was it any good?"

"It was worth doing," Ben shrugged. "You get a different perspective of the place."

"What about that park?"

"Nope, haven't been there yet. I think it's called the Minnewater. It's on our list."

Across town, the bell in the Markt began to toll. Once, twice, three times.

"Do the bells sound out of tune to you?" Ben asked.

Birdie laughed. "Yes." She held up her wrist so Ben could see her watch. "And they're off by a few minutes, too."

"Okay," Elsa called across the broad roof, "the tour continues now. We go back down these stairs. Single file and backwards is easiest."

Birdie raised her camera for one last photo of the park.

"I wish we could stay up here a little longer," she said after she'd taken the picture. She would have stayed up there all day, watching the tiny people, the flowing water and the stepped rooftops that fanned out below them. She held the warm glass in her pocket as she concentrated hard on the memory she was making and the rain-soaked fragrance of the air.

"You have time," Ben said, sizing up the number of people waiting to re-enter the stairwell. "They have to crawl down backwards so it takes a while."

"How do you know?"

"I've been here since this morning, remember?"

Movement in the park below caught the corner of her eye.

"Hey, look," Birdie said.

"What?" Ben asked.

"Down there."

A ragged-looking boy in a dark cap and a brown coat darted across the green expanse in bare feet. He seemed to shimmer, as if the heat rising from the wet ground was distorting their view. As they watched, he dipped behind a thick tree at the edge of the park and crouched way down.

He peered around the knobby trunk as a stern-looking woman dressed much too warmly for the day lumbered across a small bridge and into the park from the same direction the boy had run. She scanned the park, her irritation clear from the set of her shoulders.

She called out, but Birdie and Ben were up too high to

make out what she said.

"I think she's a nun," Ben said, leaning against the railing to get a better look. "Or else she's dressed up like one for the tourists."

On closer inspection Birdie had to agree with Ben. Her heavy clothing appeared to be long, black robes, and a broad hood lined with a white scarf cupped her face.

"She's got to be hot," Birdie said.

"I heard they do reenactments sometimes," Ben said. "Kind of like at Colonial Williamsburg but from the Middle Ages."

Birdie glanced from the boy to the nun and back to the boy. As she did, he turned his face up toward them and smiled.

"I think he sees us," Birdie said, surprised.

The boy put one finger to his lips as if shushing them and then waved.

Birdie and Ben lifted their hands in response.

"Wonder what he did," Ben said. "That nun looks mad as a rattler."

"Ben!" Uncle Noah barked. "Let's go!"

Ben jumped at his name. They turned in time to see Uncle Noah's head disappear down the stairwell. Birdie realized too late that everyone else had made their way off the roof.

"I have to go," Ben said, taking a step back and beginning to walk to the stairs.

"We both do," Birdie said as she dared one last look down at the park. "Hey, wait a minute. They're gone."

"What?" Ben was already several steps away.

"The boy and the nun. They're not there anymore."

"No way." He took a step back toward Birdie.

"Ben! Now!" His uncle's voice floated up from the stairwell.

"You'd better go," Birdie said. "Come on."

CHAPTER SEVEN

Ben followed Birdie down the spiral stairs into the cool darkness, climbing backward as everyone else had done. When they landed on the floor below they followed the murmur of voices through a small doorway that resembled a porthole and entered the next room. Elsa was talking about a series of large stone casks protruding from the walls.

Uncle Noah stood close to Elsa, listening intently. Every so often he turned an analytical eye toward the ancient equipment.

Birdie spotted her mother a few feet away from him and made her way across the low-ceilinged room with Ben close behind.

"There you are," Mrs. Blessing said as Birdie slid up next to her.

"So now," Elsa said, "the fun time starts. After all those steps you need a drink, no? Well you get one now, for free!"

Birdie looked at Mrs. Blessing, who shook her head "no" almost imperceptibly.

After a warm show of gratitude and a round of applause, the tour group bid Elsa adieu. As she left, she directed them down another set of stairs that led to a sprawling tasting room.

"Enjoy our best Bruges beer," she said warmly, "and don't forget about our wonderful gift shop."

As they made their way down the final flight of stairs, a fresh clap of thunder detonated outside, so close it made Birdie jump. The collective gasp of the tour group echoed in the spiral stairwell, followed by nervous laughter.

"I guess maybe we'll get that drink after all," Mrs. Blessing said, as rain pelted the brick tower that surrounded them. "I'm sure they have something other than beer."

They followed the rest of the group into a modern tasting room with many tables. They lined up at a long bar, where Mrs. Blessing was handed a large glass of the house beer. When the bartender began to hand one to Birdie, Mrs. Blessing intervened and ordered a cup of hot chocolate instead.

"They're a little looser about drinking in Europe than we are at home," she explained. "The drinking ages are younger and kids learn to drink responsibly with their parents. I still think it would be a bit unusual for a kid your age to sit down with a beer, though, even here. He probably wasn't really paying attention."

"Do y'all want to sit together?" Ben asked, joining them as they exited the far end of the bar after Birdie's mug of steaming hot chocolate arrived.

He pointed to a table near a stone fireplace at the far end of the tasting room. His uncle sat scrolling through his cell phone, a draught perched in front of him.

"Oh, I don't..." Mrs. Blessing began.

"Sure," Birdie said.

Mrs. Blessing raised her eyebrows at her daughter.

Birdie followed Ben, leaving her mother no choice but to come along.

They slid into high-backed chairs at the table.

"Look who I found, Uncle Noah."

"Hmmm?" he replied without looking up. After a beat of silence he lifted his gaze from his phone. He shook his hair away from his eyes when it registered that other people had joined them. "Oh, hey, how are you guys? You're from the B&B, right?"

"Yes, we're staying there," Mrs. Blessing said. "We arrived last night." She looked like she was going to begin introductions, but Uncle Noah had already resumed scrolling.

"How about that rain?" Birdie asked Ben, breaking what was beginning to be an awkward silence. "We ducked in here just in time to keep from getting drenched and now it's pouring again."

"We've been here all day," Ben said. Birdie noted the touch of fatigue in his voice. "That was our third tour."

"Really?" Birdie asked. "Why?"

"Uncle Noah's opening a brewery in Austin when we get back. They wouldn't give him a private tour on short notice, so we keep going on this tour so he can ask all his questions."

"Seriously?" Birdie asked.

Ben nodded. "We've had three tour guides so far. Elsa was the best so y'all picked the right one to go on."

"You must have a lot of questions," Birdie said to Uncle Noah.

"That I do," he replied, making a final swipe on his screen and setting the phone screen-side down on the table. He sipped what Birdie assumed was his third helping of beer. "But I think they're all answered now."

Uncle Noah took another drink and set his glass down on a colorful coaster that showcased the brewery's jester mascot.

"So, now you know my story," he said. "What brings the two of you here?"

"Not the beer," Mrs. Blessing said, setting down her glass.

"I like the hot chocolate," Birdie said. "It's fabulous."

"Oh, that's not what I meant," Mrs. Blessing said with a quick shake of her head. "The beer tastes good. This just isn't the kind of place I'd normally take you to." She turned to Ben's uncle. "As Birdie mentioned, we stopped in here because of the rain and then decided to take the tour on a whim. I did see some interesting old equipment, so it was worthwhile."

"I'm glad we came in," Birdie said. "The tour was okay and the view from the roof was amazing. How lucky was it that it stopped raining while we were up there?"

"Why are you interested in old brewing equipment?" Uncle Noah asked.

"Oh, it's not the brewing equipment specifically," Mrs. Blessing replied, lacing her fingers together. Her nails were bare and filed short. "I'm a designer so I'm always looking for interesting items. On this trip I'm studying medieval architecture and decorative arts for a new line of clothing and home accessories."

Uncle Noah didn't seem to have a response to that, so he turned to Birdie. "What grade are you in?"

"Ninth, going into tenth."

"Same as Ben," Uncle Noah said. He leaned back in the chair. "Well, we think."

Ben ran a hand through his messy crop of hair. "Yeah, I'll make it," he said. "I'm almost done with the stupid report."

"You'd better be," Uncle Noah said, picking his phone back up and scrolling again.

"Maybe if we didn't hang out in breweries all day I'd get more done."

Uncle Noah lifted his eyes from his phone. "Watch it."

"Okay, well, then," Mrs. Blessing said. She bent her

elbow to check her watch before remembering that she wasn't wearing one. "How are you coming with that hot chocolate, Birdie?"

"Almost done," she said, picking up her cup and taking another drink.

Mrs. Blessing settled back in her chair and picked up a trifold flyer that stood in the center of the table. She began to read it as she waited for Birdie to finish, but then seemed to think better of it.

"I'm going to go outside and see if the rain stopped," Mrs. Blessing said.

She returned the flyer to the middle of the wooden table. She took a final sip of beer, stood and slipped her daypack over her shoulder. "I want to make a few sketches of the brick archways leading into the old part of the brewery."

"Okay, I'll meet you out there." Birdie said. "I'm almost done."

Mrs. Blessing paused as if she were going to say goodbye to Ben's uncle, but then thought better of it.

"See you out there," she said to Birdie and left the table.

Most folks enjoy a meal at an
outside table at the Market Square,
watching all the action. I recommend
stepping off the main drag and visiting a smaller,
locally run establishment where they're less likely
to speak your language, and more likely
to have food you'll remember.

Marty McEntire's
Europe for Americans Travel Guide

CHAPTER EIGHT

The rest of the day passed quickly. Mrs. Blessing and Birdie returned their bikes to the rental shop, picked up chocolates from a shop that smelled like heaven, and walked to the courtyard behind the belfry to hear the carillon concert. They had just enough time to drop into the Church of Our Lady before it closed up tight for the day.

"I want to go back to that church again before we leave," Mrs. Blessing said as she and Birdie settled into a corner table at a café a few blocks from t'Bruges Huis. It was nearly seven o'clock and Birdie's stomach was rumbling.

"Why?"

"That statue," Mrs. Blessing said. "The Madonna and Child. It was so beautiful. So peaceful. And the details in the church itself were exquisite."

"You want to sketch."

"I want to sketch. There wasn't enough time left today to do much more than admire the statue. I want to study it."

A willowy waitress in a plaid shirt took their order. The menu was short and consisted of different versions of toasted cheese sandwiches, with or without a salad. Birdie was hungry after a lunch of fries, so she ordered spaghetti with meat sauce, which as far as she could tell, was the most filling item on the menu. Mrs. Blessing went for a toasted ham and cheese sandwich with a salad.

When the waitress left, Mrs. Blessing leaned on her elbows and looked deep into Birdie's hazel eyes. "How are you holding up, kiddo?"

Her mom didn't have to explain what she meant. She wasn't talking about the long day of sightseeing, or Birdie's tired feet, or the whisper of jet lag that still circled.

"Okay," Birdie said.

The truth was she'd been okay all afternoon. More than okay. She'd had fun exploring the town. Her heart sank when she realized she hadn't thought of Jonah once, not even when she was eating the fries. He loved fries.

"I..." But she couldn't continue.

She turned toward the window and watched the people walking by without really seeing them. The crowds had thinned considerably as the day wore on, most of them departing by bus and heading back to their tourist hotels in the bigger cities.

"What is it, Birdie?"

She didn't dare turn back to her mom. If she did, she wouldn't be able to keep the tears at bay. "I feel guilty," she whispered.

Mrs. Blessing didn't say anything. She gazed out the window, too.

"Here you go, then," the waitress said several minutes later, settling hot food in front of each of them.

"Thank you," Mrs. Blessing said. When the woman was out of earshot she said, "Come on, now, you need to eat."

Birdie nodded.

The food was hot and, despite her sadness, tasted good. They ate in silence, hungry, tired, and neither keen to talk about what they'd left behind.

It wasn't until they finished eating and a steaming cup of hot chocolate sat in front of each of them that Mrs. Blessing spoke again.

"I feel guilty, too, Birdie," she said. "Every time I smile or go hours concentrating on something else."

Birdie wrinkled her nose to keep the tears from welling in her eyes. "I don't want to forget, and sometimes I do, Mom. I forget for a little while and then when I remember again I feel awful inside. Like they will think I don't love them anymore."

"They know you love them, Birdie," she said softly, reaching across the table and taking her hand. "They know we love them. I don't think they would want us to feel awful forever."

The tears came now. She couldn't stop them. "But I should feel awful forever."

"Why is that?"

"Because it was my fault." Her voice was barely a whisper. "The accident. It was all my fault."

"The accident was not your fault, Birdie."

She squeezed her eyes closed. "Laurie Billet said it was."

"What?"

"She told the whole bus that Dad and Jonah would never have died if I hadn't wanted them at my dance recital. And she's right, Mom. If they would've just stayed for Jonah's second game, if they hadn't left the double-header to get to the auditorium in time..."

"Birdie," Mrs. Blessing said sternly. "Look at me."

Birdie opened her eyes and saw the yellow fire in her mother's hazel ones.

"Laurie Billet is an awful girl who doesn't know anything about anything. Your father and your brother wanted to come to that recital. Jonah begged your dad to leave the game early."

"He did?"

"He did. He wanted to see you, of course, but he also wanted to see Melanie. You know, Melanie? Remember her?"

"Oh," Birdie said as Jonah's choice sunk in. "He wanted to go out with her. I heard him talking to Trevor about it."

"That's right. And your dad? Your dad wanted to see you. He felt guilty that he managed to make it to every single one of Jonah's baseball games and yet always seemed to be out of town when you had something special going on. When was the last time he went to one of your school concerts?"

Birdie thought about it. "I don't remember."

"Exactly. So don't beat yourself up because the accident happened on the way to that recital. If your dad or Jonah had insisted the other way - that they stay at the game - you would have understood. It's not like you were throwing a temper tantrum to get them there."

"I was so glad they were coming, though," Birdie said. "My routine was so cool this year."

"I know it was, kiddo."

They'd never seen the routine. They'd never made it off the turnpike. They'd left the game in plenty of time, even with the slowed traffic from the bridge construction. But it didn't matter. The truck driver behind them had fallen asleep. He never even hit the brakes.

Mrs. Blessing dug in her daypack and handed Birdie a small packet of tissues. "It feels different here," she said. "I have to admit that. At home there were reminders everywhere, especially with all the packing. Here there are very few."

Birdie had tried to forget about the packing. Although a grief counselor suggested that someone else collect all of her dad and Jonah's things to donate to charity, they hadn't listened. They'd packed every last belonging themselves, even the old socks with sagging elastic they found in the back of one of her dad's drawers, even the Transformers Jonah had hidden under his bed so his friends wouldn't see them.

And they hadn't given anything to charity.

As she wiped her eyes and blew her nose, a memory drifted back, as clear as if it were happening again. She'd come home from school to find her mom sitting on Jonah's bedroom floor, in the same place she'd been when Birdie left that morning, next to a cardboard box half-filled with his clothes. She was clasping an old t-shirt to her chest and staring out his window at the swing set, lost in another day, another memory.

Birdie had taken the shirt from her hands and helped her to her feet and out of the bedroom. She settled her downstairs on the couch where she could curl up and cry like she'd done so many nights after the accident. Birdie had warmed up a can of soup for dinner and then went back upstairs and finished packing Jonah's clothes.

That box was tucked away with all the others now, labeled with a black marker and stacked in the dark storage unit at the edge of Bamburg.

And they were here.

And her mother was no longer crying.

"What are we going to do when we go back?" Birdie asked, even though a part of her didn't want to know, didn't care, didn't really want to go back at all.

"To be honest, Birdie, I'm not really sure."

"Where will we live?"

Mrs. Blessing shrugged.

"Will we be homeless?"

"No, of course not," she said, dismissing the question with a shake of her head. "I suppose we'll move back into our house if it doesn't sell, although it's much too big for us. Maybe we'll buy a little place in town or rent an apartment for a while."

"So we're going back to Bamburg?"

"I think so," Mrs. Blessing said. "I don't really want to pull you out of a school you know."

Birdie would have been okay with leaving her school, but her mom didn't know that.

"We're going to play it by ear and see what happens. We'll be overseas for the whole summer, and this is only our second day. I'm hoping our future will become clearer as our trip continues."

"That doesn't sound like you," Birdie said.

"No, I suppose it doesn't."

"You're kind of a planner, Mom."

"I'm a big planner, Birdie. I had our whole life planned. But the universe had different ideas. And now, well, now I need to let go and see what happens."

After they finished their hot chocolate, they made their way back through the cobblestone lanes to t'Bruges Huis. It was still light out, even though it was nearly ten o'clock at night. Birdie avoided looking up at the windows around them. She was glad the summer days here were so long.

Mrs. Blessing punched the code into the green panel and the front door clicked open. Birdie followed her inside.

The foyer flooded with soft light as they tripped the sensor for the chandelier.

A clash like glass hitting glass came from the sitting room.

Birdie took a step forward and looked through the archway.

A teenage girl with long blond hair and startled blue eyes stared back at her.

"Oh, hello," she said, sitting up quickly. She was definitely American. "Sorry about the noise. I just dropped my phone."

The phone in question was sitting on the coffee table

near a curvy carafe half-full of golden liquid. A puddle from an overturned glass was flowing toward it.

"You'd better grab it," Birdie said, pointing to the coming disaster.

"Oh, right." The girl retrieved the phone and then collapsed back onto the love seat. She gave the phone a once-over to make sure it was okay.

"Are you Kayla?" Mrs. Blessing asked, following Birdie into the sitting room. "We met your grandparents this morning at breakfast."

Kayla stopped fiddling with her phone. "Yes, that's me. Are you the Blessings? They mentioned you guys, too."

"Yes, that's us," Mrs. Blessing said. She glanced around the deserted sitting room. "Is anyone else here?"

"My grandparents are in bed already. Mrs. Devon only comes out in the morning. I'm not sure that she lives here, actually. I don't know about the other guests - those guys from Texas? I haven't seen them all day. In fact, I haven't seen them at all. Just heard them walking by the room." She stopped short as if she realized she was rambling.

"Okay, then, well it was nice to meet you, Kayla. Birdie and I have had a big day exploring so we're off to bed, too." Mrs. Blessing paused before she continued. "I think I saw a few clean towels on the shelf in the dining room if you need to wipe that up."

Kayla's face went a shade paler. "Okay, um, thanks."

Birdie and Mrs. Blessing climbed the narrow flights of stairs to their attic bedroom. When they were settled in Birdie asked, "Why do you think she doesn't want to be with her grandparents? They seemed nice to me."

"I don't know, Birdie. But one thing I've learned is that there is always more to things than what you think."

CHAPTER NINE

The next morning dawned bright as the last whisper of the evening's storms drifted east on the wind. Willy reclaimed the windowsill in a regal display of gray and white feathers, bobbing his head to the room before calling to his companions across the sleepy city.

"Morning, Willy," Birdie said, as she snuggled deeper into the cocoon of her yellow duvet. "Thanks for the wake-up call."

She would have liked to stay in bed for a while longer, watching Willy and gazing at the sun breaking over the red stair-stepped rooftops across the street. But it was not to be. Her mother had already left the room for the morning, which meant she was probably late for breakfast.

The thought of missing Mrs. Devon's wonderful cooking provided the burst of energy she needed to climb out of bed.

She showered and dressed before joining her mother in the dining room. When she arrived, she found Mrs. Blessing alone at the neatly set table studying a tiny porcelain bowl. She turned it over in her hands and read something written on the bottom.

"Good morning," Birdie said, sliding into the same chair she'd sat in the day before.

"Good morning," Mrs. Blessing said, setting the bowl next to her plate. "How did you sleep?"

"Good."

"No dreams?"

"None that I remember," Birdie said.

"Good." Mrs. Blessing plucked the white linen napkin that stood like a three-cornered hat from her plate, shook it out gently and placed it across her lap. She was wearing faded jeans and a heather green t-shirt.

Birdie examined the tiered serving tray in the center of the table. Each layer was artfully arranged with breads, pastries, jellies, jams, and small jars of plain white yogurt.

She reached for a yogurt and a tiny container of raspberry preserves.

A rumble on the stairs signaled Ben's arrival.

"Good morning," he said, crossing the sitting room and folding himself into the seat next to Birdie. He reached for two pieces of cinnamon-nut bread and the butter dish.

"Well, good morning to you, too, Ben," Mrs. Blessing said.

"So what did y'all do last night?" he asked, using a small knife to apply a thick layer of butter to the bread.

"We met Kayla," Birdie said.

"Really? I was beginning to wonder if she even existed," Ben said good-naturedly before taking a large bite of the cinnamon-nut bread.

"Oh, she exists, alright," Mr. Hinnershitz said, entering the room through the sitting area. "She's just in a different time zone than the rest of us."

He took a seat across the table from Mrs. Blessing.

The pocket door slid open and Mrs. Devon emerged from the kitchen.

"Good morning, everyone," she said, bustling around

the table as she poured coffee for Mr. Hinnershitz and Mrs. Blessing. "Would anyone care for an egg this morning?"

"That would be wonderful," Mrs. Blessing said. "What about you two?"

Birdie opted for a boiled egg with toast and Ben asked for a three-egg omelet.

"With cheese?" Mrs. Devon asked.

"Yes ma'am," Ben said.

"And toast I think?"

Ben nodded. Mrs. Devon smiled warmly and returned to the kitchen.

"So, any big plans for today?" Mr. Hinnershitz asked.

"Oh, it looks like a great day for the canal cruise," Mrs. Blessing said.

Mr. Hinnershitz nodded his approval, and then, although Mrs. Blessing had not requested it, launched into a detailed explanation of the procedure for finding the dock, buying the tickets, and boarding the boat.

Ben leaned in close to Birdie.

"Do you have the aventurine?" he asked.

Birdie nodded and retrieved it from the front pocket of her jeans.

She rubbed its smooth surface with her thumb. As she did the golden flakes shimmered and began to move.

"Whoa," Ben said under his breath. "It's doing it again."

Birdie handed the piece of glass to Ben. His breath caught when he touched it. "It's getting warm."

"See," she said, "it's nothing like those toys at the brewery."

"What's it making?" he asked as he balanced the glass on his open palm under the table between them.

The sparkles quickened and began to take shape. They collided into streams of golden light, swirling and undulating before driving together into a perfect image.

"Holy crow that's hot," Ben said, placing the aventurine

on the seat beside him and rubbing the palm of his hand on his tan cargo shorts. He examined the newly formed picture on the glass. "What is that?"

"I think it's a knight," Birdie said, as surprised as Ben sounded. "You know, like from a chess set?"

Ben examined it closely, but didn't handle the hot glass again.

"Do you play chess?" he asked.

"I never learned," she replied, shaking her head. "But my brother had a chess set in his room at home. He and my dad..."

"You have a brother?" Ben asked, raising his eyebrows in surprise.

Birdie realized too late that she had said too much.

"I..." she began.

"What do you two have there?" Mrs. Blessing asked, looking around Birdie to see what was sitting on the seat next to Ben.

"It's a toy," they both said at once. They looked at each other. Ben laughed.

"You owe me a pop," he said.

Birdie covered the aventurine with her hand. It had cooled enough to handle and she slipped it back into her pocket.

"What's so funny?" Mrs. Hinnershitz asked as she made her way across the sitting room and took the seat next to her husband.

The pocket door slid open and Mrs. Devon returned with an egg in a dainty cup for Birdie and, for Ben, an omelet so large that its edges slipped over the side of the plate.

"There you go," she said. "*Bon appetit.*"

With the arrival of Mrs. Hinnershitz the conversation shifted away from Birdie and Ben, and back to plans for the day. Even Ben seemed distracted from his question by the size of the steaming breakfast before him.

Birdie examined her egg, which was sitting upright, still in its shell. A spoon so small that a sugar cube would dwarf it sat on the flowered saucer under the cup.

Birdie picked up the tiny spoon and knocked it into the top of the egg.

Nothing happened.

She hit the egg again, this time a bit harder, but it still didn't crack.

"Should've got an omelet," Ben said, spearing his fork into a hunk of egg and cheese.

Mrs. Devon returned with plates for Mrs. Blessing and Mr. Hinnershitz and took Mrs. Hinnershitz's order before going back to the kitchen.

"What are you and Birdie doing for dinner tonight?" Mrs. Hinnershitz asked Mrs. Blessing as she extracted a large fruit and cheese danish from the middle tier of the serving rack.

"I don't know. We haven't made any plans yet."

"You could join us if you'd like. Couldn't they, Harry? We'd love the company. We're going to the oldest pub in town. It's called *Herberg*-something. It's about half a kilometer away, right Harry?"

Mr. Hinnershitz nodded. He, too, had opted for the three-egg omelet and was enjoying it wholeheartedly.

"Marty says it's an easy walk," Mrs. Hinnershitz continued. "And it's supposed to be like going back in time. It celebrated its 500th anniversary a few years ago."

"What do you think, Birdie?" Mrs. Blessing asked.

"Okay by me." She still had not succeeded in removing the egg from its shell.

"Oh, that's good. Let's plan to meet in the sitting room at 6:30 - I'm sorry, I mean 18:30 - and we can all walk over together," Mrs. Hinnershitz said. She turned to Ben. "You're welcome to join us, too, Ben, and your uncle of course."

"Thank you, ma'am," Ben said, but he sounded doubtful. "I'll ask."

As the women discussed the pub they'd visit that evening, Birdie set the useless spoon back on the saucer and picked up a large, heavy butter knife from beside her plate.

Crack!

That did it: the weight of the knife made a dent in the top of the shell. She used her fingers to remove the chalky white fragments and then carefully cut the egg open with the knife.

"Mom."

Mrs. Blessing paused half way through a sentence and looked over at her.

"Oh, that's okay, it's a soft-boiled egg. Just dip some toast in there."

Mrs. Blessing resumed her conversation.

Birdie looked at Ben.

He shrugged. "Should've got the omelet."

After breakfast, Birdie and Mrs. Blessing gathered their daypacks and headed through the sunny cobblestone lanes to a small wooden dock where they bought tickets for the next canal cruise. They waited in line and then squeezed onto a long, narrow boat with a couple dozen other tourists. They were helped aboard by a young man with clipped blond hair and a golden tan who turned out to be their captain.

As Birdie shoved her ticket stub into her pocket, her fingers lit on the small piece of glass. She took it out and turned it over in her hand. The gold wasn't moving anymore, and the chess piece held firm when she rubbed it.

The open boat jerked sideways as two men pushed it away from the dock. Birdie quickly slipped her hands into her jacket pockets before the aventurine could fly into the canal. She held it tight to be safe.

The boat settled slowly under the weight of its passengers and then floated gently into the canal. The captain fired up the engine and the boat began to crawl through the languid water.

He recited a well-rehearsed script, first in Dutch, then in French, and finally in English. After the first few trilingual explanations, Birdie found it hard to pay attention. She tuned him out and instead studied the view of the medieval city from this lower angle, noticing the docks and the doors that backed up to the water.

They passed under several low stone bridges, ducking their heads each time. They rounded a bend and waved at a group of tourists waiting in line for a cruise at another dock.

Further on, Birdie spotted a group of boys playing in a clearing a few yards from the stone wall that lined the canal. They were dressed as if they were going to one of the historical reenactments Ben had told her about. She wondered if they were the same kids she'd seen bopping through Burg Square the day before. It was hard to tell from this distance, but she thought these boys looked younger.

They were playing some kind of game, hurling rocks at a stake in the ground. As the boat drifted closer to the bank, Birdie realized it wasn't a stake at all, but a bird that had been buried so only its head stuck out from the dirt.

She gasped and twisted away from them.

"Mom, did you..."

"They all give the same tour," Mrs. Blessing said, clearly focused on the guide's commentary rather than the grisly game being played on the canal bank. She leaned in close to Birdie so the captain wouldn't hear her. "The city regulates how much they charge and what they can say. That's what Marty says, anyway."

Birdie lost sight of the clearing as the boat made a wide, slow U-turn at a point where two canals intersected.

Had she really seen what she thought she saw?

Who would do that?

As they began the slow ride back down the canal, Birdie scanned the bank for the clearing with the boys, but when they passed by it again she saw only a handful of tourists wandering through.

She started to wonder if her eyes were playing tricks on her. Perhaps she'd imagined the boys, or misinterpreted what she saw. Who would do such a terrible thing to a bird?

She thought of Willy, bobbing his head on their windowsill that morning.

It must have been a toy. That's the only explanation that made sense. The tourists would have stopped the boys if they saw them hurting a poor defenseless bird.

She settled back against the hard bench and closed her eyes for a moment to push the image from her mind. Then she took a deep breath of humid air and opened them again.

The cruise continued, passing back under one of the bridges and beyond the dock where they boarded. Mrs. Blessing seemed lost in thought as she studied the buildings that rose up on either side of the canal.

As they approached another low stone bridge, Birdie spotted a sandy-haired boy with an odd-looking hat leaning over the side. The reflection of the sun off the water made him kind of shimmer, and he seemed to be staring right at her.

As they drew closer, Birdie realized that he looked like the boy she and Ben saw from the brewery roof the day before. He wore the same dark cap and clothes that were too heavy for the day. Behind him, a horse pulled a tourist carriage with an elderly couple perched on a seat in the back.

The boy was definitely staring at her.

Birdie pulled her hand out of her jacket pocket and

waved.

He smiled broadly, and then waved in return.

The boat had nearly reached the bridge when his smile faltered and he turned his head as if he'd heard a loud sound. Birdie scanned the bridge to see what had distracted him, but nothing seemed obvious.

Without turning back to her, he sprinted from the bridge on bare feet, disappearing into the thickening crowd.

"Wait!" Birdie cried, half-standing.

"Birdie! Sit down!" her mother said, grabbing her jacket and pulling her back into the boat. "You'll get your head knocked off by one of the bridges. What were you thinking?"

"I..." she began, but she was drowned out by the captain's monotone narrative as he continued in a language she didn't understand. He paused and switched to English.

"On the right side..."

Birdie hunkered down and scanned the canal bank for the boy.

There was no sign of him.

The boat slowed when they reached another broad intersection and reversed course, heading back the way they'd started.

She almost stood again when she caught sight of him a few moments later, sprinting up the front steps of a red brick house with purple and red blooms tumbling from its window boxes. He slid through a sliver of open door and then was gone.

She twisted in her seat to watch the house as they passed by.

A tabby cat wove a lazy circle on the stoop and then sat down. Curtains were drawn tight behind the window boxes on each floor, except for a single window under the eves, where they were pulled wide.

Birdie could have sworn she saw a little girl looking down

at her from the window in the eves.

She blinked and looked again. The girl was still there, but faded back into the room like a shadow.

The canal boat sounded its horn, a crass beep that startled everyone on board.

Birdie looked to see what the problem was but it wasn't immediately obvious.

It didn't matter anyway. The house was behind them now, out of sight around the bend.

Birdie sighed heavily as she settled back onto the crowded bench and waited for the cruise to end.

CHAPTER TEN

"What did you see back there?" Mrs. Blessing asked as they made their way off the dock. "You scared the heck out of me."

"Sorry, Mom. I saw a boy," Birdie said. "He waved to me."

"Was it Ben?"

"No, someone local I think. He was younger than Ben and dressed in heavy clothes. We saw him yesterday from the brewery roof, too."

"Ah, that explains why it took you so long to rejoin the group."

When Birdie didn't respond Mrs. Blessing said, "Maybe you could sketch him."

Birdie stopped walking and looked at her mom. "That's a good idea. But I'm not sure..."

"There," Mrs. Blessing said, pointing to a shaded green bench not far from the bridge where the boy had stood. "We could sit there for a while."

"...I can draw him."

"You'll never know until you try," Mrs. Blessing said

with a shrug.

They made their way through the crowded street to the empty bench and sat down.

Birdie tugged her sketchbook from her daypack and opened it wide across her lap. She pointed her toes against the cobblestones to level the book on her legs, then paged past the scenery she'd sketched to a crisp, blank page. She carefully selected colored pencils that most closely matched her impression of the boy, the sandy hair and dark coat, the pale skin and dirt-stained shirt.

To her surprise and relief the drawing came easily, as if she were sketching from somewhere deep inside to conjure his image. In the picture he stood on the bridge with one bare foot perched on the stone curb, his pale face lit with a slight smile as he stared at something in the distance.

When she was done she placed the last pencil into its pouch and considered her work.

It was the best picture of a living, breathing human being she'd ever sketched.

"No shoes?" Mrs. Blessing asked, taking a break from her own sketch to study Birdie's drawing.

Birdie shook her head and closed her sketchbook on his bare toes.

"You don't have to stop."

"I'm done for now," she said. She leaned over and looked at her mom's work. "What are you working on?"

Mrs. Blessing pointed down the canal to an arched window towering above the tall doors of a cathedral. It was several blocks away, but Birdie could make out the scrolled metal work that caught her mother's attention.

"Nice," she said.

"Oh, it's okay," Mrs. Blessing said. She closed her sketchbook, too. "I need to spend more time drawing to really capture what I'm seeing. I feel like I never spend more than a few minutes on anything. There are so many distractions everywhere."

She pulled her camera from her daypack, zoomed in and took a photo of the window.

"Like that," she continued, pointing to the place she'd just photographed. "I keep finding these interesting arches and windows. I'm just not capturing the feeling of them very well. And the photos don't do them justice. I feel like I need to get one right before I move on to other things."

"Well, we could go back to Mrs. Devon's and you could do some drawing before dinner," Birdie said.

"You wouldn't mind?"

"No."

"But there are so many more things to see." She began rummaging in her daypack. "Marty McEntire listed..."

"Mom, it's okay. Really." She reached out and touched her mother's hand.

To Birdie's relief she dropped the guidebook she'd started to extract back into the pack.

"I do like the idea of an afternoon of drawing," she said, her hazel eyes meeting Birdie's.

"Isn't that why we're here? So you can come up with designs?"

Mrs. Blessing nodded.

"Let's go then."

When they arrived at t'Bruges Huis, Birdie punched in the code on the keypad and they stepped inside. The sitting room held the still air of solitude that settled on an empty house.

"We can eat at the table," Mrs. Blessing said, lifting the bag of sandwiches they'd picked up at a café on their way back to the bed and breakfast.

It was strangely quiet sitting at the table without the companionship of the other guests. They finished quickly, cleaned up their trash, and then moved back into the sitting room.

Mrs. Blessing sat in a high-backed chair and placed her materials on the end table beside her. Birdie settled onto the love seat and propped her feet up on the coffee table.

"Birdie, please."

She lowered her sneakered feet and opened her sketchbook to the page with the boy.

He stared back at her, his smile wide, his old-fashioned pants revealing skinny ankles.

Who are you? she wondered.

She selected pencils in two shades of brown and began to fill in more of the details, the dirt on his feet, the creases in his billowy white shirt.

The house was silent except for the scratching of her mother's charcoal on the porous paper and the slow tick of the tall grandfather clock that loomed against the wall. Sunlight pooled on the floor and disappeared as clouds passed by outside.

"Mom?" Birdie asked a long while later when she had done as much work as she could on the sketch without ruining it.

"Hmmm?"

"Do you feel like going for a walk?"

Mrs. Blessing didn't look up from her page. "Not right now, no. I'm kind of in the zone."

Birdie closed her sketchbook and placed it on the table with her pencil pouch. She stood up and stretched in front of a large fireplace with the hulking marble mantle. On either side hung portraits of a man and a woman. They did not smile. Their dark clothes were enriched with lace collars and sleeves. They were the most uncomfortable-looking clothes she'd ever seen. She couldn't imagine wearing a lace collar the size of a life-preserver around her neck. How could they have possibly thought that was fashionable?

"Let's go."

Uncle Noah's voice was muffled by the front door, but he was speaking loudly enough that Birdie heard him clearly. Mrs. Blessing looked up from her drawing and they exchanged a surprised glance.

"What's your problem?" Ben asked, matching his uncle's volume.

"You're the problem, Benny. You need to get your crap together."

"I finished the damned paper, okay? I sent it off last night."

"Late."

"It was not late. I had until tomorrow to get it done."

"It was due back in May."

"I had an extension."

"That's the problem." The door cracked open as Uncle Noah continued, his voice growing louder. "You always expect special treatment."

"I do not." They were in the foyer now, facing off.

Mrs. Blessing cleared her throat.

The effect was immediate.

Uncle Noah stiffened.

"Oh, hey," he said, turning to Birdie and Mrs. Blessing.

Mrs. Blessing offered a curt nod and returned to her sketch.

Birdie's stomach sank at the look of pure mortification that passed across Ben's angular face.

Uncle Noah turned back to Ben and scowled. "I'm going upstairs to get some work done. Unlike you I don't have an extension. I need to get the business plan done or there won't be a business. That's how it works in the real world."

Ben stood motionless in the foyer watching his uncle trudge up the stairs. They all heard a door close louder than it should have when he reached the hallway above them.

Ben seemed to be debating his next move.

"Do you want to go for a walk?" Birdie asked him,

making her way across the sitting room and out into the foyer where he stood. He looked like he was about to bolt out the door anyway.

"Yeah," he said gruffly. He didn't meet her eyes. "Sure."

"Mom, do you mind?"

Mrs. Blessing looked up from her sketchbook and sighed.

"No, I don't mind. Are you sure your uncle will be okay with it?"

"Who cares?" Ben asked. "Not him."

"You might be wrong there," Mrs. Blessing said.

They stood silently for several moments.

"Well, go ahead then. Don't be long. We'll need to get ready for dinner with the Hinnershitzes in about an hour."

"Thanks, Mom."

"And watch for cars," she said as the charcoal touched the paper. "They drive up these narrow lanes like maniacs."

There are many lovely parks
in Bruges to take a break from
all the action. One particularly
beautiful spot is the Minnewater,
a park and "lake of love"
near the Begijnhof.

Marty McEntire's
Europe for Americans Travel Guide

CHAPTER ELEVEN

"Are you alright?" Birdie asked Ben after they'd closed the door and made their way to the cobblestone alley up the street.

"Yeah, I'm alright." He released a pent-up breath as he ran his long fingers through his disheveled hair. "My uncle doesn't trust me."

"Oh," Birdie said.

"Yeah."

They walked on without speaking. They hadn't gone far when they heard a fast rumble behind them. They stepped up onto a tiny curb just in time to avoid a small black taxi barreling up the alley.

"It's my parents," Ben said, breaking the silence as they stepped back down onto the cobblestones. "They sent me here with him. They told him I'm a bad kid and that I needed to get away from Marshall Falls."

"They really said that?"

Ben nodded.

"You didn't want to come?"

"Not really. But now that I'm here it's kind of cool, you

know? But Uncle Noah just can't let it go."

"Didn't he want you to come?"

"He said he did, but, hell, I don't know. He doesn't act like it."

"He seems pretty busy with the brewery thing."

"Yeah."

They'd emerged from the alley onto a lane bordered on one side by a stone wall overlooking the canal. Ben leaned over the wall and stared into the water below.

"Any fish?" Birdie asked.

"I don't see any."

They watched the water for a while.

A tourist boat passed beneath them.

"Hey," Birdie said. "I didn't get a chance to tell you. I saw that boy again."

Ben stopped leaning on the wall and stood up straight. "You did? The one from the brewery?"

"Yep. I saw him when my mom and I were on the canal cruise this morning. He was on one of the bridges we passed under. And get this, he waved to me again."

"No way."

"Way. But then he ran away."

"Which way did he go?" Ben asked, looking up and down the canal as if the boy would appear.

"Uh, well, let me see," Birdie said, getting her bearings. "We got on the cruise at that end of town and then traveled past here and up by the church." She pointed to the church up the canal at the far end of the bend. "Then we turned around and came back past here. He was on the second bridge up there, I think. Then he ran off heading in that direction." She pointed to the other side of the canal bank. "I caught sight of him again going into one of the old houses that front the water."

"Let's go," Ben said. He started off at a fast clip and Birdie had to jog to catch up to him.

"Where?"

"To his house."

"Why?"

"Why not?"

"I'm not sure I can find the place again," she said.

"Well, let's go check it out anyway."

They followed the lane along the canal until they reached the second bridge. As they crossed it, Birdie could hear the narration from the tourist boat passing beneath them.

Ben stopped. "Okay, which way?"

Birdie pointed to the right and they took off down another cobblestone lane.

"This is hopeless," she said several minutes later, realizing that she had no idea where she was. She stopped jogging. "Everything looks the same."

"This isn't it?"

"No, I don't think so."

"Well, hell," he said. He studied the buildings around them as if they'd provide a clue.

"Let's keep going," Birdie said. "Maybe we'll find a hotel or a bike shop with a map."

They walked to the end of the lane, but didn't see any place that might have a free map. As they neared another intersection, the lane opened into a park with tall trees and a manicured lawn.

"Look," Birdie said, pointing to a tall red brick building.

"That's the brewery."

"Yep. And this must be the park the boy was in. What did they call it? The Minnewater? It was something like that."

"There," Ben said, pointing to a thick tree near the canal. "I think that's where he was hiding."

They crossed the park and circled the tree.

"Check it out," Ben said, looking up. A new group was

perched on top of the brewery, admiring the view of Bruges from the rooftops.

Birdie smiled. There was probably some kid up there watching them, although the distance was far enough that she couldn't make out anyone's face in particular. She could tell that some of the people were shorter than others, and some wore more colorful jackets while others were dressed in black. But she couldn't make out facial features.

She wondered if the tourists could see her better than she could see them, maybe even as clearly as she had seen the boy the afternoon before. Perhaps it was a trick of the light and the clouds. Nevertheless, she placed her fingers to her lips, just as the boy had done, then ducked down, smiling. Now someone else would have a mystery kid to try to find.

Birdie's smile didn't last long after she turned away from the brewery and began to examine the space behind the tree.

"Look at this," she said, gesturing to a place on the ground that had been scuffed.

Ben bent down to examine the dirt.

Birdie's eyes drifted from the scuffed marks to the roots. Her breath caught.

"Ben."

He followed her gaze. There, under a delicate web of soft leaves and grass clippings, lay a package wrapped in paper and twine, barely visible under the greenery. It was small, not much larger than Birdie's outstretched hand.

"What is it?" he asked.

Birdie reached down and picked up the package.

"It's heavy," she said. "And a little damp."

"Open it," Ben said.

"It doesn't belong to us."

"So? Finders keepers."

Birdie unwound the twine and pulled the thick leaves of paper away.

"It's a book," she said.

"Let me see."

The volume was bound in deep brown leather and tied shut with a thin strip of cowhide. The cover held no words, but a stamped knight was embossed on the smooth material. Birdie recognized it at once. It was the same chess piece that appeared on the aventurine that morning.

"Whoa," Ben said as Birdie examined the cover.

"It looks old," Ben said.

"It feels old," Birdie said, handing it to him.

"It must weigh three pounds," he said.

She fished the small piece of glass from her pocket.

"Do you think it was his?" Birdie asked.

She held the aventurine next to the book. The images were identical.

"Well, I didn't notice a book when we saw him from the roof, but we were pretty far away. Did he have one when you saw him on the bridge?"

"I don't think so, but that doesn't necessarily mean..." Birdie began as she slipped the stone into the pocket of her jeans.

"I know, but it's still interesting." Ben handed the book back to her.

"It's not wet. If he'd dropped it while we were on the roof it would be soaked from the storm."

"He had it tucked under those leaves pretty good," Ben said.

"Still," Birdie cradled it in the crook of her arm protectively. "What do you think we should do with it?"

"Nothing for now," Ben said, looking around to make sure they weren't being watched. The group on the brewery roof had descended the stairs. "Here, wait, give it back to me."

Birdie hesitated.

"Don't you trust me?"

She studied his deep brown eyes for a moment and then handed him the book.

Ben pulled open the Velcro flap of the bottom pocket of his cargo shorts and slipped the book inside. It just fit, although it significantly weighed down the side of his pants.

"That's not obvious," Birdie said.

"No one will be looking for it," Ben said. "So they'll just think I brought a guide book along."

Birdie considered his answer. "Good point." She checked her watch. "Oh crap, we've got to go. Let's take it back to the house and open it."

When they arrived back at the bed and breakfast, they found a welcome committee waiting for them in the sitting room. Mrs. Blessing had been joined by Mr. and Mrs. Hinnershitz, who were sitting in the armchairs across from her enjoying a glass of the golden liquid from the carafe that sat in the middle of the coffee table. Kayla, who was clearly not enjoying a glass, was standing near the fireplace studying her phone.

Uncle Noah was pacing the small room.

"Hey," Birdie said as they came in and the conversation faltered. "Are we late?"

"Where did you go?" Uncle Noah exploded toward Ben.

Mrs. Blessing exchanged glances with the Hinnershitzes. They were trapped. There was no way out of the sitting room without stepping right between Ben and his uncle.

"For a walk," Ben answered, rising to his full height.

"Mr. Martin," Birdie said, stepping in front of Ben. "It was my fault. I asked Ben to go for a walk with me. I was bored and I asked my mom but she was busy." She cast a look at her mom that said she was sorry for dragging her into this.

"She's telling the truth," Mrs. Blessing said from her place on the love seat. "I told them it was okay."

"What right do you have to tell my nephew what he can and can't do?" Uncle Noah asked, turning on his heel to confront Mrs. Blessing.

"Now, calm down, son," Mr. Hinnershitz said.

Mrs. Blessing rose to her feet, lifting a steadying hand to silence Mr. Hinnershitz.

"You will not speak to me in that tone," she said to Uncle Noah, her eyes latching on to his. "You were not here when the decision was being made. My daughter wanted to go for a walk and I trusted your nephew, who has been nothing but courteous and kind to us - which is more than I can say about you, by the way - to accompany her."

Uncle Noah opened his mouth but no words came. His deep eyes, so fiery a moment before, became unreadable.

The silence stretched.

Even Kayla stopped swiping her phone long enough to take in the situation.

Birdie held her breath.

"Sorry," Uncle Noah mumbled.

Mr. Hinnershitz stood and crossed the room. He slapped a round arm around Uncle Noah's shoulders.

"What do you say we head over to the pub a little early," he said jovially. "We can make sure everything's set for dinner before everyone else arrives." He turned to Birdie and Ben. "You kids need to get cleaned up, right? Ben, can you escort the ladies to the pub when they're ready?"

No one said anything.

Birdie considered kicking Ben's sneaker to get him to respond.

Mr. Hinnershitz looked at Ben hard, lifting his bushy eyebrows and his chin expectantly.

"Yes, sir," Ben said quietly. "Will do."

Birdie could feel the tension begin to slip from the room.

"Very good. We'll see you there then," Mr. Hinnershitz said, his mustache concealing his upper lip as he nodded his approval.

Uncle Noah and Mr. Hinnershitz left without saying anything more. After the door clicked closed, Mrs. Hinnershitz shooed them away with a sweep of her hand.

"Well, you heard the man, go get yourselves together."

Birdie and Ben escaped up the stairs.

Ben paused in front of his door on the first landing.

"I'm sorry," Birdie whispered, feeling guilty that she's asked him to take the walk with her.

"Do you want the book?" he asked at the same time.

Neither spoke for a moment.

"Ah, don't worry about it," Ben said, deliberately keeping his voice low so they wouldn't be overheard. "I needed a walk to cool my head."

Birdie nodded. "That's true enough."

"What about the book? Do you want it?"

"No," she said, shaking her head. "You can hold onto it. We'll look at it later."

Birdie left Ben on the landing and continued up the stairs to the third floor. When she reached the door to the room, she rummaged in her jeans pocket for the key. Her fingers landed on something warm and smooth instead. She pulled the aventurine from her pocket and looked at it.

The golden knight stared back at her. She rubbed the glass but the chess piece held firm.

CHAPTER TWELVE

The café hugged the curve of a cobblestone street near a gently flowing canal, its whitewashed brick facade punctuated by red trim. The placard above the door noted the name and date of establishment: 1515.

Birdie, Ben and Kayla followed Mrs. Hinnershitz and Mrs. Blessing through a paneled foyer, past faded photographs and paintings, and into a dark pub. In one corner, a wooden bar gleamed with the polish of centuries of spilled drinks, while near the fireplace a handful of men in shorts and polo shirts leaned on a wooden table. They held rounded snifters of beer under the watchful eye of the original proprietor, whose portrait stared down at them.

They followed a server through the pub, down a spiral staircase and into a hidden courtyard garden. Birdie spotted Ben's uncle and Mr. Hinnershitz on high-backed stools at one end of a long, high-top table near what looked like a horseshoe pit.

Mr. Hinnershitz raised a hand in recognition when he saw his wife and the others emerge from the stairwell. The group wove through a hodgepodge of tables and chairs that were sheltered from the evening sun by brown umbrellas.

"Well, there you are now," Mr. Hinnershitz said, rising as they arrived at the table. Uncle Noah half-stood, too, although it seemed like he wasn't sure why. By Birdie's measure he appeared in better spirits than when he'd left t'Bruges Huis.

Birdie, Ben, and Kayla arranged themselves on tall stools at the opposite end of the table from the adults, leaving several open seats between the two groups.

Ben avoided his uncle's eyes.

"How was your walk?" Mr. Hinnershitz asked after the women sat down.

"It was good," Mrs. Blessing said. "The later it gets the less people there are to wade through."

"That's the benefit of sleeping over, isn't it?" Mrs. Hinnershitz said as she adjusted her large frame on a stool beside her husband. "The mornings and evenings are ours."

"You know, the guidebook says..." Mrs. Blessing began.

Kayla sighed, pulled her phone from her daypack and began swiping.

Birdie leaned closer to Ben. "So what did you do with the book?"

"Brought it," Ben said, patting the enlarged pocket of his cargo shorts. "Thought we might get a chance to look at it."

Birdie waited until a waiter took their drink order and the adults resumed their conversation before she continued. "Let's see it."

Ben tugged the book from his pocket and held it on his lap below the table. He checked to make sure no one was watching them and then passed it over to Birdie. She glanced up at her mom, but she was absorbed in Mrs. Hinnershitz's description of a tour group and their selfie-sticks.

Birdie found it curious that Uncle Noah was not looking at Mrs. Hinnershitz as she spoke, but instead seemed to be studying her mother.

"Are you going to open it?" Ben asked.

Birdie turned her attention back to the book in her lap.

She was once again amazed by the weight of the volume. She unwrapped the paper covering. The golden knight stared back at her.

She pulled the aventurine from her pocket and compared it to the book.

"Identical," Ben said.

Birdie nodded. "Should I open it?"

"If you don't, I will," Kayla said without looking up from her phone. "What's the big secret, anyway?"

Birdie slipped the glass back into her pocket.

"No secret," she said.

The waiter returned with their beverages and jotted their food order on a small tablet, beginning with Mrs. Hinnershitz and working his way around the table.

"Maria, can I talk to you for a minute?" Uncle Noah asked after the orders were taken. He gestured toward the stairs that led up to the pub. Mrs. Blessing nodded and they excused themselves.

Mr. Hinnershitz waved them away good-naturedly and then winked at Ben.

"What was that?" Birdie said under her breath.

"No clue," Ben said between his teeth as he nodded and smiled at Mr. Hinnershitz.

Mrs. Hinnershitz pulled her Marty McEntire book from her bag and nudged her husband.

"Hmmm? What? Oh yes." He lifted his snowy eyebrows at her. "Yes, yes. We should plan for tomorrow."

When Birdie was certain the Hinnershitzes were not in the least bit interested in what she was doing and her mother and Ben's uncle were otherwise occupied, she tugged on the rawhide string that held the book cover closed.

It gave way with a small puff of dust and leather.

The cover was heavy as Birdie opened the book, minding the binding and the soft pages beneath.

"It's really old," Ben said.

"Yes, but…" Birdie examined it closely.

"What's wrong?" Ben asked.

"I don't know. It's weird. It looks ancient, but it feels new."

"What do you mean?"

"Well, look at the leather cover." She held it out so he could feel it. "It's soft and new, but I've never seen a book bound like this before. Have you? And the pages," she flipped through them gently, "they're soft, not brittle like I expected them to be. I figured they might crumble when I touched them, but they didn't. And the ink is vibrant, too, not faded or running with age."

"Maybe it's a reproduction," Kayla said without looking up. "There's a bookstore near t'Bruges Huis that has all kinds of new books that are reproductions of old ones. We went there the other day and my grandparents bought one about the ancient city of Troy or something." She shrugged. "It's a tourist thing."

Birdie opened the cover.

The first page was blank.

She turned to the second page.

"*The Game and Playe of the Chesse*," she read, deciphering the peculiar script she found there. She looked up at Ben who was also studying the words on the page. "It's an instruction manual."

"In really old script," he said. "That's almost impossible to read."

"Almost, but we could probably make out some of it."

"At least it's in English," Kayla said. "Could be French or Dutch and then you'd really be up the creek."

"Okay, so why did that boy have the book, and why was

that woman chasing him?" Birdie asked.

"Stole it," Ben said, sitting back on his stool. He laced his long fingers behind his head as he leaned against a wall of ivy-covered bricks that rose up behind him. "I bet you a hundred bucks he stole it from that store Kayla's talking about and that nun figured it out and was trying to get it back."

Birdie had to admit it made sense. "Unless..."

Ben raised his eyebrows at her.

"Unless," she continued, "he is trying to learn to play chess."

"From an ancient English instruction manual that you can barely read?" Ben said.

She twisted her lips, searching for an alternative theory. She drew a blank.

"Okay, so now we have stolen property," she said, closing the book and sliding it back to Ben. "Great."

"I hear the prisons here aren't so bad," Kayla said. "Besides, they'd stick you two in juvie anyway."

"I guess we should take it back to the bookstore," Birdie said, ignoring Kayla. "And tell the owner what happened."

"Hold on now," Ben said, sitting forward and leaning an elbow on the wooden table. His shaggy bangs fell across his eyes and he swept them out of the way. "We don't really know what happened, do we? We've got a theory, but..."

"Well, we could at least go to the store and see if they carry this book," Birdie said. "Kayla, how far is the bookstore from the bed and breakfast?"

"A few blocks. Not far at all. It's by the gelato shop." She pointed over her shoulder in the general direction of the store. As she did, Mrs. Blessing and Uncle Noah emerged from the pub and came down the stairs. They crossed the garden to reclaim their seats at the table.

Birdie tried to catch her mom's eye but Mrs. Hinnershitz had already caught her attention.

Uncle Noah picked up his glass of beer and took a drink.

"So now, tell me about that beer you're drinking," Mr. Hinnershitz said.

The four adults at the end of the table reminded Birdie of a painting. Their faces were animated in the golden light of the fading sun, framed by the red brick wall of the building behind them that crawled with ivy and brightly colored blooms. She took a mental picture and closed her eyes to lock the details into her brain.

"We can see," Ben said as he wrapped the book in its paper cover and put it back in his pocket.

"What?" Birdie asked.

"The bookstore?" Ben reminded her. "We can see if we can go. But I'm not sure Uncle Noah will let me out of his sight tomorrow. I've never seen him as hot as he was this afternoon."

"Ask him tonight while he's drunk," Kayla offered without looking up. "They usually say yes when they're drunk."

Birdie considered Kayla's suggestion. She decided she was glad she didn't know if it was true.

Ben laughed but there was no humor in it. "You don't know my uncle. He doesn't get drunk. I know he talks a big game about beer all the time and he tries a lot of different types, but he usually goes for small samples and doesn't really drink that much."

Birdie looked at Uncle Noah's glass. It was barely a quarter of the size of Mr. Hinnershitz's glass.

"See what I mean? It's a sample. He'll probably try one or two more and then call it a night. He's trying to learn about beer, not be annihilated by it."

"Are they free?' Kayla asked, sizing up Uncle Noah's glass.

"What? The samples? Sometimes, but I think he usually has to pay something. Sometimes he can't get the sample size, like when we were at the brewery. He had to take a full size beer there, so he just didn't drink it all. Apparently there are laws here that you can only serve beer in a glass with the brewery or the brand stamped on it. There are all different shapes and sizes of glasses depending on the type of beer, and not every company provides sample sizes."

Kayla nodded, clearly impressed with Ben's knowledge.

"Well, then we'll have to ask him about the bookstore when my mom's around," Birdie said bringing the subject back to the matter at hand. "That might make a difference."

Ben nodded. "Worth a shot."

Birdie sipped her soda and waited for the dinner to arrive. She didn't realize how hungry she was until the steaming plate of spaghetti with meat sauce was placed before her. A basket of fresh bread and butter appeared a few seconds later.

"How is it?" Mrs. Blessing called from the other end of the table.

"Awesome," Birdie said, and meant it even though she was beginning to wonder if she would eat spaghetti every night.

Mrs. Blessing nodded and dug into her soup and toasted sandwich.

Dessert followed dinner as the daylight began to fade.

"It's got to be late," Birdie said, looking up at the sky.

"I wonder how much longer they're going to want to stay," Ben said.

"Hey, do you guys mind if we walk back to the B&B?" Kayla called up the table.

The adults exchanged glances.

"I'd prefer if you stayed here and walked back with us," Mrs. Blessing said. "It's getting late."

Uncle Noah and the Hinnershitzes nodded in agreement.

Kayla scowled and lost herself in her phone again.

Ben and Birdie settled back onto their stools.

At least they had a plan.

An hour later the sun's last orange ribbon slipped across the canals into moonlit darkness as Ben and Birdie trailed the others back to the bed and breakfast. They'd kept themselves occupied at the pub playing *bowles* in the horseshoe pit, which the waiter explained was a game where each player rolled heavy stone wheels toward a stake in the ground to see who could get them closest. Birdie and Ben had managed to hit both the stake and several of the tables that surrounded the pit.

Deep shadows stretched across the narrow lanes, broken only by occasional puddles of light from the lantern-like street lamps. Birdie shoved her hands in her jacket pockets. She cupped the aventurine in her fingers and felt it grow warm.

A few blocks away church bells rang out a hymn to close the day.

They were nearly at t'Bruges Huis when Birdie saw him.

"Ben," she whispered but he didn't hear her over the chimes.

She squinted to make out the figure in the dark.

She pushed on Ben's arm. "Do you see him?"

Ben slowed and followed Birdie's gaze down the alley that led to the canal wall they'd sat on that afternoon. Half way down the block, a sandy haired, barefooted boy in pants that were too wide and long at the same time sat with his legs dangling over the edge of the wall. A blanket of fog hugged the water behind him, casting a shimmering glow that lit the night.

They stopped. The others continued on, deep in conversation.

"It's him," Birdie breathed.

"I see him," Ben said. He allowed a quick glance at the

grown-ups. "They'll hear me if I call to him."

Birdie nodded in agreement.

"What should we do?" he asked.

Birdie lifted her hand to wave. As she did, the boy jumped from the wall and started jogging toward them.

"He's coming," Birdie said, drawing in her breath. "I can't believe it. Ben, he's coming."

"I can take him," Ben said, adjusting his stance.

Birdie placed a hand on his clenched fist and lowered it. "Of course you can. He's half your size. Let's hope that won't be necessary."

Ben relaxed a little and Birdie dropped her hand. The boy was barely three houses away now.

"Ben!" Uncle Noah barked. Ben jumped and reformed his gangly fight stance, only this time pointed up the cobblestone lane toward his uncle.

Birdie turned just in time to see her mother shush Uncle Noah. She recognized the action, Jonah having been on the receiving end of it so many times.

Birdie held up her index finger. "Just a sec," she whisper-yelled back.

"Now," Uncle Noah bellowed, ignoring Mrs. Blessing.

Birdie felt Ben tense beside her.

"It's okay," she said. "Go."

"What about you?"

Birdie turned back to the alley. "I'll talk to..."

But the boy was no longer moving toward them. He was running the other way.

"Wait!" Birdie cried, no longer caring who heard her.

But the boy didn't wait, and a moment later he reached a curve along the wall and faded out of sight.

"Let's go," Ben said. "Son of a...." He kicked at the cobblestones and started walking.

Birdie watched the spot where the boy had disappeared for a moment longer, and then fell into step beside Ben.

"Don't get into it with your uncle," she said. "I'm too tired to listen to it and if you tick him off he won't let you come to the bookstore with me tomorrow."

Ben shot her a disapproving look and then softened.

"Yeah, whatever," he said. "I don't need a fight either."

When the adults saw them on their way, they resumed their pace toward the bed and breakfast. Kayla, for her part, stayed halfway between the two groups, as if she were too cool for the grown-ups and too old for Ben and Birdie.

"We should follow him," Ben said. He was staring at his uncle's back several yards in front of them.

"What? We already are."

"No, not Uncle Noah. That kid. We should sneak out tonight and figure out where he went."

"No way," Birdie said.

"Why not?"

"What if we get caught?"

"I won't be in any worse trouble than I am now."

"But I will be," Birdie said. "Besides, we don't know where he went."

Ben shrugged. "He probably went home."

"Maybe," Birdie said. "Hopefully."

"Hey," Ben said, pausing as if he were going to turn back. "Do you think you could try to find his house again?"

"Right now?"

"No," Ben said. "Tomorrow. When we go to the bookstore."

"If you can go."

"Yes, if I can go."

Birdie thought about it. "I don't know. I got all turned around this afternoon when we tried," she said. "We'd need to go back to where my mom and I were on that canal cruise. The streets and the houses look so much alike it's hard to tell them apart. The lanes in this town are so confusing."

Uncle Noah checked to make sure they were still following them.

"Come on," Birdie said, resuming her pace. "Things always look brighter in the morning."

CHAPTER THIRTEEN

"So what do you know about chess?" Ben asked his uncle the next morning at breakfast. He'd made his first appearance at Mrs. Devon's table since Birdie and her mom arrived.

"The basics. It's a strategy game." Uncle Noah reached across the table to retrieve a tiny jar of yogurt and two pieces of toast from the stacked tray in the center of the table. "Complicated, but once they understand how to play people seem to enjoy it."

"Do you know how to play?"

"I learned in fifth grade, so let's just say I'd be a little rusty. It's a game where every kind of piece makes its own moves. Some can only move forward, some only sideways, some only diagonally. You have to play a lot to get the hang of it." He took a generous bite of toast and chewed it before addressing Mrs. Blessing. "What about you? Do you know how to play?"

"I do," she said.

"Really?" Birdie asked.

"Really."

Birdie drew a blank at first, but then an image fought its way to her mind as if it were floating up to her from deep sleep.

She remembered the weathered wooden chessboard now. It sat on a table on the sprawling front porch of a lake house in upstate New York. How long had it been? Five years? Yes. It had been the summer of fourth grade.

Everything was so different then.

They'd spent a lot of weekends away before everything changed, most of them tied to Jonah's baseball tournaments.

While she and Jonah tossed a ball back and forth at the water's edge, their parents had played chess, laughing and drinking white wine that was so clear the sun sparkled through the tall glasses.

Jonah had been rough with the hard ball, throwing it to her like she was one of his teammates. She'd pretended it was fine, but the palms of her hands stung at the memory.

Then, to her horror, her eyes began to sting.

"You okay, Birdie?" Uncle Noah asked, pausing part way through an explanation of the moves that the queen could make.

She cleared her throat, nodding as she pushed the memory away and willed the tears not to fall. "Yep, I'm good. I just forgot that my mom knew how to play, that's all."

"Do you know what moves the knight is allowed to make?" Ben asked as if he hadn't heard his uncle's question.

"Hmmm," Mrs. Blessing said, leaning forward to study Birdie before turning her attention to Ben. "I'd almost need a board to show you. The knight moves sort of diagonally, but it has to land on a different vertical or horizontal line than it's already on. Here. Look."

"It's also the only piece that can leap over other pieces," Uncle Noah said as Mrs. Blessing tried to show them the proper movement using yogurt jars and glasses of juice.

Mrs. Devon entered through the pocket door and raised her eyebrows at the makeshift game board.

"Oh, this is no good," Mrs. Blessing said, returning each item to its proper place.

"I'm sure we'll come across a chess board somewhere on this trip," Uncle Noah said. "I'll show you then."

Mrs. Blessing leaned in close to Birdie as Uncle Noah talked to Ben.

"It's okay, Birdie," she said softly before straightening again. "So today," she continued at her normal volume, "we're going to visit the Jerusalem Chapel and the Lace Museum. That shouldn't take long if we get there before the crowds. Then I want to go back to Burg Square to do some final sketching, and then probably take one more stroll to make sure we didn't miss anything fabulous before we leave for Germany tomorrow."

"Wait, we're leaving tomorrow?" Birdie asked, the chessboard forgotten.

"Yes, that's the plan. I think we've seen about everything here, haven't we? We hit all the highlights in the Marty McEntire book for sure."

Birdie began to nod but then Ben said, "Except for the bookstore."

Birdie looked up at him hopefully.

"No, I don't think Marty mentioned a specific bookstore," Mrs. Blessing said. She paused, thinking. "Well, I take that back. Maybe he did. I kind of remember seeing a list of places that sell his guidebooks."

"I'm not sure, ma'am. But Kayla told us there is this really cool bookstore in town," he said.

"This from the kid who turned in his book report a month late," Uncle Noah said, sitting back in his chair and draping a long arm across the empty one next to him.

Ben ignored him. "We were talking about it at dinner last night. We were kind of hoping to go see it."

Mrs. Blessing considered them for a moment.

"Well," she said drawing her attention back to Uncle Noah, "What are you two up to today?"

"I'm picking up a rental car in," he pressed the button on his phone to see the time, "thirty minutes. Then we're heading out to the Westvleteren Abbey."

"What's at the abbey?" Mrs. Blessing asked.

Uncle Noah gave her a withering look. "It's only considered to be the place where the very best beer in the world is brewed."

"Oh," Mrs. Blessing said. "Of course it is. And it's housed in an old abbey?"

"Monks make the beer," he said. "There are quite a few monastery beers brewed in Belgium and in other places across Europe. It's an old tradition that makes them money."

"And I bet we're fixing to see them all," Ben said under his breath.

"Most of them," Uncle Noah said cheerfully, tipping his glass of orange juice at Ben in a toast. "But Westvleteren is the toughest to get into. They don't want people disturbing the monks."

"Do I have to go?" Ben asked.

"What else will you do?" Uncle Noah said. "Besides, you'll get to see some of the countryside and learn how the monks brew the beer. It's only about an hour away."

Ben did not look happy at this suggestion.

"Well, if you don't mind tombs and lace, you're welcome to explore the town with Birdie and me today. We could make a point of stopping at that bookstore," Mrs. Blessing said. "With your uncle's permission, of course."

"Oh, of course," Uncle Noah said, the corner of his mouth twitching as he tried not to smile.

"Can I?" Ben asked.

It was a moment before Uncle Noah responded.

Birdie held her breath.

"Sure, Ben. You can stay here with Birdie," Uncle Noah said without taking his eyes off Mrs. Blessing. "As long as Mrs. Blessing is sure she doesn't mind."

"Well that's great," Mrs. Blessing said, picking her napkin up from her lap and wiping the sides of her mouth to hide her own smile. "We'd love the extra company. When do you expect to be back?"

"With the tour and the drive probably not until about six tonight."

"Very good," Mrs. Blessing said. "We'll be sure to be back here then so we can deliver Ben safely back into your care."

Ben coughed as his orange juice went down the wrong pipe. Birdie slapped him hard on the back and he stopped sputtering.

"Problem?" Uncle Noah asked him.

Ben swallowed. "No, sir."

"Then thank Mrs. Blessing for offering to let you hang out with them today."

"Thank you, Mrs. Blessing."

"You're welcome, Ben."

The rest of the breakfast passed quickly. Uncle Noah finished his meal, handed Ben some money for lunch, and then excused himself to catch the taxi Mrs. Devon had arranged for him to pick up the rental car. Ben waited in the sitting room while Mrs. Blessing and Birdie went upstairs to get their daypacks. Ten minutes later they were standing in front of the towering brick steeple of the Jerusalem Church. It was capped with a giant green orb supporting a small cross and flanked on each side with a spire. One spire was topped by a golden sun, the other by a golden moon.

"There's nobody here," Birdie said, turning in a circle to peer down each of the curved lanes around them.

"Perfect," Mrs. Blessing said, pulling out her sketchbook.

Birdie and Ben followed her under a brick archway beside the church and into a formal garden where they found a ticket booth and entrances to a small museum, a coffee shop, and the church. Ben handed Mrs. Blessing a few heavy coins and she bought three tickets.

They visited the garden and museum first, then headed toward the church. It was much smaller than the Church of Our Lady, and Ben had to fold himself nearly in half to get through the low-slung door leading into the sanctuary. Even Birdie had to duck.

Inside, the sun shone through windows that rose all the way to the top of the tall steeple. The brick walls were adorned with woodcarvings and paintings of the Madonna and child. A black marble tomb rose up from the middle of the floor, with a man and woman sculpted onto its surface. The woman wore a traditional Dutch dress and hat that reminded Birdie of a witch's costume, and a dog lay under her feet. The man wore armor with a lion under his boots.

Beyond the tomb, a stone altar was carved as if it were an excavation site, with bones, skulls, lanterns, rope, and tools protruding from its surface. Candles flickered before it.

Ben and Birdie followed Mrs. Blessing through a passageway behind the altar and down a short set of stairs into another chamber.

On the far end, a wrought iron gate stood open.

The gate was even shorter than the door had been and Birdie ducked low to make her way through it. Inside, behind a decorative metal grate, a life-like sculpture of a nearly naked Jesus lay on a slab staring toward heaven from beneath his crown of thorns.

"What is this place?" Birdie asked, suddenly overcome with the thought that the sculpture might open its eyes and start talking to them, or worse, reach through the metal grate that surrounded it and grab her ankle. She took a step back and bumped into the brick wall.

"It's a replica of a church in Jerusalem that was built over Christ's tomb," Mrs. Blessing said.

"Why?" Birdie asked as Ben bent down low to check out the savior's face.

Mrs. Blessing tugged her guidebook from her bag and turned to a dog-eared page near the front. She held it near one of the candles so she could see the text. "This says that the man who built it was very faithful and traveled to Jerusalem in the 1400s when not many people would have done such a thing." She closed the book. "So he built it to show his devotion to God."

"Oh."

"Good thing he did, too," Ben said, standing up as far as he could, which wasn't very far. "Apparently the original one was destroyed."

"How do you know that?" Birdie asked. For a split second she wondered if the sculpture had whispered it to him, but she shook the thought away.

"Saw it in the Marty McEntire book," Ben said, gesturing to the one in Mrs. Blessing's hands.

Birdie raised her eyebrows at him.

"What?" Ben said, spreading his hands wide. "Do you have any idea how many breweries we've been to? I needed something to do to keep from going crazy."

"So you read Marty McEntire books?"

Ben shrugged. "It was that or the book about all the breweries."

"What about the book for your report?" Birdie asked.

"Very funny," Ben said.

"Okay," Mrs. Blessing said, checking her watch. "Why don't you two go into the coffee shop and have some hot chocolate. I just have a few more things to sketch in here. I won't be long. It looked like there were some comfy couches in there."

She didn't have to tell them twice.

Thirty minutes later with two stomachs full of cocoa and one sketchbook full of drawings, they made the short walk to the lace museum. They started at the gift shop and ticket desk, which sat on the ground floor of a large, walled-off building, which was surrounded by a lush garden like the church had been.

"I would love to learn how to make this lace," Mrs. Blessing said, holding a piece up and examining its intricate design in the sunlight that came through a tall casement window.

"There's a class," Birdie said.

"There is?"

Birdie pointed to a bulletin board that hung nearby.

Mrs. Blessing studied the flyer that listed the class information.

She shook her head.

"I don't think that's going to work." She checked her watch. "The class starts in about five minutes but it lasts all afternoon. We'd never make it to the bookstore and we haven't had lunch, not that I'm very hungry after Mrs. Devon's breakfast, but..."

"You could stay, Mom, and take the class, and Ben and I could go to the bookstore and then stop somewhere for lunch."

"Oh, I don't know," Mrs. Blessing said, glancing around the shop before settling her gaze on Ben. "What would your uncle think?"

"I don't think he'd mind, do you Ben? It's okay with me, anyway," Birdie said. "Really. I'd much rather get a chance to see that bookstore than learn to make lace."

Mrs. Blessing looked at Ben again. "What about you?" she asked.

He held up his long, crooked fingers. "Ma'am, I don't

think these hands were built for lace making."

Mrs. Blessing laughed. "Okay then. I'll stay and take the class and you two can go to the bookstore and get some lunch. You can take your time because I won't be done until after five. You can meet me back at the bed and breakfast."

She dug into her pocket and handed Birdie some money and her wrinkled map. "Stay together. Don't talk to strangers. And be careful. Watch where you're going. Do you know where you're going? The drivers..."

"Are maniacs. I know, Mom."

"Yes, of course you do. But still..."

"We'll be careful and I think we can find our way. Kayla said the bookstore isn't far from the bed and breakfast."

"Okay. If you're sure." Mrs. Blessing gave Birdie a quick hug and headed toward the registration desk. She was almost there when she turned around.

"Oh, and have fun," she said, a smile lighting her face.

"Thanks, Mom."

"Now we can go try to find the boy's house," Ben said as soon as they were back outside and making their way down the cobblestone lane that curved around the Jerusalem Church. "You said you thought you could find it if we went back to the place where you and your mom went on the canal cruise."

"Did you bring the book?" Birdie asked.

Ben patted his weighed down pocket.

"We can try," Birdie said. "But I'm not making any promises."

They made their way back to t'Bruges Huis and then retraced the route she and her mom took to the dock the day before. There were entrances for canal cruises all over town and Birdie wasn't sure she'd find the right one unless they went all the way back to the beginning.

The lanes grew increasingly crowded as they wound

their way to the entrance.

"We're almost there," Birdie said.

Ben looked around as if he expected to see the boy run past.

"There's the bridge," Birdie said, pointing to the stone arch near the bench where she'd sat to draw his picture.

They climbed to the center of the bridge and stepped to the side to allow the other tourists to pass. The wide canal flowed silently beneath them, broken only by the rumble of the tourist boats.

"There," Birdie said, pointing at one as it slid smoothly from beneath the bridge. "That's the way we went, too. Do you see the spot with the small dock? The canal curves there and you can't see what's around the bend."

Ben nodded.

"That's where the buildings start again. That's where I saw him go into a house."

They crossed onto the narrow lane that bordered the canal and followed it until they reached the bend. As Birdie predicted, the green space gave way to tall houses.

"They all look so similar," she said, shaking her head. "It's hard to say which one it was."

They continued down the narrow lane for a short distance before Birdie stopped again.

"Wait," she said, taking a seat on the wall next to the canal. Ben stood beside her, one sneakered foot propped up on the stones.

Birdie surveyed the houses that hung together along the canal.

"Only some of them have flowers," she said.

Ben shrugged and spread his hands apart, asking what that had to do with anything without saying a word.

Birdie studied the flowers that tumbled from the window boxes.

"Ben, that's it! That's the one." She pointed to a narrow

red brick house that rose three stories from the canal. She cocked her head as she considered the facade. "Only the flowers in the window boxes are a different color. They were purple and red yesterday. I thought it was such an odd color combination when I saw him go in."

"I'm not seeing any purple flowers, Birdie."

"They're not purple now. They're pink and yellow. But I recognize the coats of arms painted on the window boxes. Come on, let's go."

"But..."

"Just trust me."

Ben shrugged and followed her.

You'll find flowers at every turn
throughout Europe, and
Bruges is no exception.
Homeowners and businesses
take pride in the colorful displays
that grace window boxes and planters
no matter what time of year you visit.
During the winter holidays,
watch for evergreens to
take the place of the
pansies, petunias and begonias
that brighten the spring
and summer months.

Marty McEntire's
Europe for Americans Travel Guide

CHAPTER FOURTEEN

They stepped up to the arched wooden door of the red brick house. Birdie raised a tentative hand to knock but stopped when she noticed a long iron rod hanging from the side of the shallow roof that covered them. She pulled it gently, then harder when nothing happened.

A heavy bell clanged inside.

"Here, you hold this," Ben said, extracting the book from his pocket.

They waited for what felt like a terribly long time. They exchanged disappointed glances. Ben nodded toward the rod and Birdie reached to pull it again. She stopped midway when she heard movement behind the door. Ten seconds later a metal lock scraped and the door eased open little more than a crack.

A woman who was nearly as tall as Birdie stood behind it. Her gray and white hair twisted in heavy curls that wanted to float away from her head. Her eyebrows were the same mix of color, long and twisted, but stopped short of combining into one. Her nose and ears were long with age, and her light blue eyes were hooded by heavy lids.

The woman stared at Birdie and Ben but didn't speak. Birdie's mouth went dry.

"Pardon, ma'am," Ben said in creaky Dutch. "Specht Engels?"

The woman tilted her head up sharply to inspect Ben, then nodded. She didn't speak.

"We are ... we found this book," Ben said, switching to English. He pointed to the paper-wrapped volume in Birdie's hands. Birdie loosened her grip on the package and unwrapped the paper, revealing the golden knight on the cover. "We thought it might belong to the boy who lives here."

The old woman eyed Ben suspiciously.

"No boys live here," she said, her voice a light soprano, startling in its contrast to her heavy appearance.

"But ... oh, but are you sure? I saw him the other day," Birdie said, stepping forward. "He came in through the front door."

"Yes, I am sure there are no boys living in my house. I am sorry my dear, but you are mistaken," she said, staring hard at Birdie. "There are no children here."

"But..." Birdie hesitated as the woman's eyes grew wide. "But I could have sworn ... and there was a little girl, too, up in the gable window."

The woman chuckled and shook her head. The effect on her hair made Birdie think of a gray and white feather duster picked up in the breeze.

"There have not been any children here since I was a young girl myself. I am sorry, but you must have the wrong house."

"We're sorry to have disturbed you, ma'am," Ben said, taking a half step back and tapping Birdie's elbow.

The woman considered them for a moment. Then she said, "Oh, no, no problem at all." She smiled, revealing lightly yellowed teeth. "You are American?"

"Yes," Ben said as Birdie nodded.

"We were on the brewery roof," Birdie said, "and I thought I saw a boy who lived here at the park. Then we found this book and ... I'm really sor..."

"Oh, I said it is no problem," the woman said, lowering her heavy lids in a way that told Birdie not to apologize again. "But since you did ring my bell, would you care to join me for some tea?"

She pulled the wooden door open expectantly.

Ben began to say no but Birdie interrupted him.

"Yes, thank you, that would be lovely."

They crossed the threshold into a vestibule. The old woman closed the solid front door behind them and then opened a second door that was taller than the first. It had two brightly colored stained-glass panels that caught the light from the room beyond. One showed a yellow lion with a green tree and the other a white standing bear.

They followed her through a small foyer with an accent table, and into a tastefully decorated parlor with two high-back chairs and a dusky blue love seat. The furniture sat on a woven rug with a polished wooden table in the center. A porcelain tea set sat in the middle on a silver tray. It reminded Birdie of the sitting room at t'Bruges Huis.

"Please sit down," she said, gesturing to the well-worn chairs. She picked up the tea service. "I will heat the water."

Ben and Birdie exchanged glances as they settled into the tall chairs.

"Why did you say yes?" Ben whispered after the door to the kitchen had closed behind the elderly woman.

Birdie leaned in close. "This is where those kids were. I'm sure of it."

"Well, they're not here now," Ben whispered, gesturing to the empty room.

"I know that, but maybe we can learn something useful. We could show her the book."

Ben shrugged and gave her a look that said he thought they were wasting their time.

Birdie didn't bother to argue with him. She examined the room instead.

A carved mantle above the brick fireplace came alive with flowers, cherubs, fairies and vines. An aged photo of a young couple in their wedding clothes sat on top next to a small box made of blue and gold wood. An elegantly curved mirror reflected the room back to them, capturing the molding that outlined the painted ceiling. Even their own reflections seemed faded and out of time in the aged glass.

Beneath their sneakers sat a woven rug unlike any Birdie had seen before. It was more like a tapestry than a rug, with round storybook vignettes. One section showed a mother and her children in a field, another a father in black clothing, and a third, angels in heaven welcoming them all. There were other scenes, too, but they were hidden under the furniture.

Birdie picked up her feet and looked at the soles of her sneakers. The last thing she wanted to do was drag dirt onto the rug. She always took her shoes off at home. She hadn't even thought to do it here. Until now.

"Here we go," the woman said, coming back into the room through the swinging door. "Fresh and hot."

She set the heavy platter down on the table and placed a dainty cup and saucer in front of each of them.

"Now," she said as she poured the steaming black liquid into their cups. "How do you take your tea?"

"Usually with milk and sugar," Birdie said, thinking of the only other time in her life she'd had tea.

"And you, young man?"

"The same way, please, ma'am," Ben said.

Birdie stifled a giggle that was working hard in her throat. The tiny teacup looked ridiculous in front of Ben, like he was playing tea party with a bunch of dolls.

But this was no party.

Birdie closed her eyes for longer than a blink and steadied herself.

"Aha," the woman said, and fixed the tea for them without another question.

Birdie didn't know the proper way to take tea, and she would have bet money that this was the first time in Ben's life he'd even had a cup.

Birdie reconsidered the woman who was pouring their tea. She wore bright coral slacks and a coordinating sweater, with a lovely pendant necklace falling on her speckled chest.

Birdie silently admonished herself for her first impression of the woman, which had been so dark and heavy. Now, in the parlor, fresh tea steaming in front of them in the bright light streaming through the lace window sheers, she looked like a nice old lady.

"So, now what is it that brings you two to Bruges, all the way across the ocean from America?" she asked.

"I came with my mom," Birdie said. "She's a designer. She's developing a new medieval themed line of clothing and home accessories and wanted to visit different places in Europe for ideas."

"I see," she said, turning her attention to Ben. "And this great designer, she is your mother, too?"

"Oh, no, ma'am," Ben said. The teacup looked like a toy in his giant hands. It tittered against the saucer as he spoke.

"You are not brother and sister then?"

Birdie gulped and Ben answered. "No, ma'am. We just met at the bed and breakfast."

"Oh, I see. Fast friends then? Which bed and breakfast might that be?"

"t'Bruges Huis," he said. "A woman named Mrs. Devon owns it."

"Certainly. I know Mrs. Devon well. She is the niece of

my good friend Alma, God rest her soul. Alma died last year. Did you know?"

Birdie and Ben looked at her blankly.

"No, no, of course you didn't. Sad story, really. I'm not sure they ever did find the taxi driver who hit her. She was crossing over Steenstraat with a bag of apricots from the Wednesday market and then, well, you know the rest I suppose."

The woman took a long sip of the steaming tea, leaving a bright slash of coral lipstick on the rim of the white cup.

Birdie didn't dare to look at Ben.

"And what have your done so far in our fair city?" the woman asked after she swallowed.

"A lot," Birdie said. She listed the sites she'd visited with her mom. "And we went to the brewery, too, and took a bike ride to the windmills."

"Yes, well, we are known for our great brewery. Did you know it is the oldest in the area?"

"Yes," Birdie said. "Our tour guide told us all about it."

"Oh, good. Who was your guide?"

"Elsa," Birdie said.

"Oh, you were lucky then. She is the best one, in English anyway. My husband always requested her for his tour groups, God rest his soul. Not that we had many Americans then. No, not many at all. A few. Mostly the English speakers came from Great Britain, although sometimes the Germans preferred the tour in English if they wanted to practice the language. There were the Chinese tourists, too. Sometimes they took the English tour, but never as part of my husband's groups. They brought their own tour guides from China."

She smiled at them over her cup and took another sip. She gripped the cup with gnarled fingers on both hands. Birdie noticed three rings on each hand, each one with a different brightly colored stone.

"And what about you, young man? You've been awfully quiet. What brings you to Bruges?"

"My uncle brews his own beer at home, and he's thinking about starting a brewery of his own," Ben said. "So we're here so he can try different types across Europe."

"Hmmm. Across Europe? Well, Belgium has the best beer in all of Europe, he will find. Not that I partake much myself. I prefer tea."

"That's what he said, too, about Belgium, I mean." Ben smiled. "But he feels the need to try beer in several countries just to be sure."

The woman chuckled. "Yes, yes, of course he does. If you believe what you read in the newspaper, though, it is the United States that has the best breweries. Loads of little ones springing up all over the place."

"That's what Uncle Noah wants to open," Ben said. "A little one. They call them craft breweries."

"Yes, yes, that is right. You are absolutely correct, young man."

She studied them a moment.

"And what are your names?"

"I'm Ben."

"Birdie."

"Ah, good names to be sure. I am Mrs. Olinda Winggen."

Although they may seem unapproachable,
don't be afraid to ask a local for advice.
Learn a few words in their language
and chances are they'll be more
than willing to give you
the inside scoop on their
favorite places.

Marty McEntire's
Europe for Americans Travel Guide

CHAPTER FIFTEEN

"Mrs. Winggen, when we were on the porch you said you've lived here since you were a little girl," Birdie said.

"Yes, indeed I have. I've lived here my whole life. First with my parents, then with my husband, Alan, before he passed, God rest his soul." She pronounced her husband's name *uh-lawn*.

"Is that the two of you?" Birdie asked, pointing to the wedding photo on the mantel.

"Yes, dear, that it is. Many years ago." She twisted her lips as if she were thinking hard. "Let's see. It would have been sixty-two years now, if he were still alive."

Birdie thought about the photograph of her own mother in her white wedding gown, her arm wrapped warmly around her father in his black tuxedo, smiling like Mr. and Mrs. Winggen. It was too sad to consider how short their marriage had been.

"Your house is very nice. Has your family always owned it?" Ben asked after a moment of silence as they all looked at the photograph.

"Oh, not always, no," she swished the silly idea away

with her bejeweled fingers, "but we've had it for, oh, let me see." She glanced up at the painted ceiling as if it held a clue. "The past five hundred years, I suppose."

Ben and Birdie exchanged glances.

"Before that it belonged to a merchant who traveled to Venice from time to time. He was quite wealthy and was the leader of one of our guilds. The guildsmen were in charge of everything back then as you know, I'm sure. He built and staffed this house for his wife and family. We were the two big places back then, Venice and Bruges."

"Five hundred years?" Birdie repeated.

The woman smiled, taking another sip of tea. "Ah, yes. Five hundred, give or take a few. My family took charge of the house after the merchant and his wife succumbed to the plague. So sad. She was French. His wife, I mean."

"French?" Ben asked.

"Yes, we mixed things up back then with the French and the English. But still we kept our Dutch heritage here in Bruges. There were many languages spoken back then. There still are, I suppose. It is one of the reasons we get so many tourists. But that is just my opinion."

"You speak English so well," Ben said.

"Yes, yes, I suppose I do. I helped my husband in his business, God rest his soul."

Birdie sipped her tea as she listened to Mrs. Winggen. It was hot and bitter on the tip of her tongue, despite the sugar and cream. It was nothing like the tea she had before, which had tasted strongly of cinnamon and was a million times sweeter than what she was currently drinking. But that tea had been part of an elementary school project where they dressed up and pretended to be on the Titanic, so her teacher must have sweetened it up so the kids would drink it.

"Do you like the tea, dear?" Mrs. Winggen asked, setting her own cup on its saucer. "Do you need another lump of sugar?"

Birdie nodded and Mrs. Winggen dropped another cube of tan-colored sugar the size of a Monopoly die into her dainty cup. She gestured to Ben with the sugar grabber.

"And you, young man?"

"I'll take three more," he said.

"Thank you," Birdie said softly as she stirred the dissolving cube in her tea.

"So, Birdie, tell me about this book you found," Mrs. Winggen said, as she poured herself another cup. "You said you thought it belonged to a boy who lived here? Yes, too bad. The last time a boy lived here it was my own father, and before that, his father. It has been, oh, I would say at least a hundred years since anyone who you would consider a boy lived here."

"Were you an only child?" Ben asked.

"I had a sister, a few years older than me, but she passed, God rest her soul," Mrs. Winggen said. "I do have two daughters of my own, and someday they will live here. Or at least one of them will. They'll need to work that out, I suppose. After five hundred years the house must stay in the family, don't you agree? Besides, they loved it here when they were little girls."

"Where are they now?" Ben asked.

"Brussels, working, raising their own children. I see them from time to time. Not much work here in Bruges unless you cater to the tourist trade. Alan did make a good living on tourism, you understand, brought tour groups here and the like. Put the girls on a good path in life. We had fun back then, taking the people around. It wasn't like today, no. Now everyone with a credit card and a Marty McEntire book comes traipsing through. Back then only those with real money vacationed in a forgotten city like Bruges."

"Why do you call it that? Forgotten?" Ben asked.

"Oh, well, because it was you see. After the port silted up

the merchant ships stopped coming. People moved away to find work or they died from the plague. For hundreds of years it was as if Bruges didn't exist at all as far as the rest of the world was concerned. But then, in the 1800s, the artists and painters - they were the romantics you know - yes, they discovered our charms and riches and we became a stop on the grand tour that aristocrats took when they came of age."

She picked up her teacup. "My daughters will probably retire here, if I had to imagine. It is a lovely place to live, out of the bustle of the big city, as long as we can keep the tourists in check."

They sat quietly for a moment, sipping their tea. Birdie's was much better with the extra lump. Ben also seemed to be drinking his more easily with the extra sugar.

"Mrs. Winggen," Birdie said. "When your husband ran the tour company, did he ever hear of a special piece of glass from Venice? It's called aventurine."

"Ah, yes, aventurine," she replied, setting her teacup down and eyeing Birdie curiously. "A fool's quest if ever there was one. They sell replicas of them in the gift shops around town. Every so often I see a young person with one. A whole lot of rubbish if you ask me."

"So you don't believe in the legend?" Ben asked.

"Believe in magic?" she huffed. "Of course not. Now don't misunderstand me, Bruges feels like a magical place, of course, because of its history and beauty, so people think there is more to it than that. But there is not. The only real magic here is in the imaginations of the tourists."

She lifted the kettle from the tray and topped off her teacup.

"Now, Alan, he believed," she said.

"Your husband?" Ben said.

"Yes. He believed in the legend of the aventurine completely. I think he adored the idea of going back in time for real, not just talking about the past to his tour groups."

"You must miss him," Birdie said.

"Indeed."

They sat quietly for a while, sipping tea.

"So, tell me more about this book you found," Mrs. Winggen reminded Birdie, nodding to the leather bound lump in her lap.

"We found it under a tree in the park near the Begijnhof," Birdie said. "I think a boy dropped it there when he was running from one of the nuns."

The woman chuckled. "Oh, now, I cannot begin to imagine one of the Benedictine sisters chasing a child through the Minnewater. That's the name of that park, the Minnewater."

"Oh," Birdie said. "It looked like he was hiding from her."

She settled her empty teacup on its saucer on the coffee table.

"Is there any chance a boy and girl live nearby?" Ben asked. "Maybe Birdie got the house wrong."

Birdie was certain this was not the case, but she chose not to correct Ben in front of Mrs. Winggen. Besides, the woman had already made it clear that she found their tale far-fetched.

"I'm afraid not," Mrs. Winggen said, wrinkling her brow until her multicolored eyebrows almost met. "Half of the houses are vacant and for sale - at crazy prices if you ask me - and the others are owned by older people like me or rented out like Mrs. Devon's. No children."

"Oh." Ben looked disappointed.

"What is the book about?" Mrs. Winggen asked, trying again to bring the subject back around. Her blue eyes sparkled in the sun that filtered through the lace window sheers. The pattern of the light reminded Birdie of her mother several blocks away learning to weave lace by hand. She would kill her if she knew they were in some stranger's house sipping tea.

"Chess," Birdie said quietly. "It's an instruction manual."

Mrs. Winggen gave her an odd look. It was several moments before she spoke.

"Perhaps the book has the boy's name inside the front cover," she finally said. "People do that sometimes, especially with leather-bound books that are expensive or private. They want to make sure the book gets back to them if it is lost."

Birdie glanced down at the book in her lap.

Her eyes narrowed.

The embossed knight that had been so bright and gold when they stood on the doorstep now held only faint hints of color, pale reds and greens, perhaps a touch of what was once yellow. It looked different than it had at the pub.

"Why don't you open it and check," Ben encouraged her.

Birdie reached down and tugged at the rawhide that held the book closed.

The small bow held tight, not wanting to pull free.

"Is it stuck?" Ben asked, leaning forward and looking like he might get up to help.

Birdie grasped the rawhide at a spot closer to the bow and pulled harder. It scratched through the knot and, with a small spray of dust, came undone. The rawhide fell onto her lap, still wrapped snuggly around the back of the book. Birdie turned it over and noticed that it was secured there by what looked like a series of small belt loops. She hadn't noticed them before.

She opened the front cover, which held tight as if it had never been opened before.

The first page was yellowed and blank.

Birdie turned it as gently as she could.

Centered on the second page a handwritten paragraph appeared in a careful, elegant script.

Birdie stared at it, amazed. She would have sworn that page wasn't there when they opened the book at the pub the night before.

Birdie couldn't make out the handwritten words.

"Is his name there?" Ben asked.

She held the book out to the woman. "Mrs. Winggen, can you read what this says? I think it's in Dutch."

"Let me take a look." Mrs. Winggen pulled a thin pair of reading glasses from the pocket of her sweater and put them on. She accepted the book from Birdie and held it open about a foot from her face, squinting at the curlicue script through the colorful plastic frames.

"No, dear, I don't think this is Dutch. It may be, I don't know, could it be Celtic? Celtic, yes, that could be it," she said, "which, unfortunately, I do not know."

"Well, that's strange," Ben said. "Why would there be a book written in Celtic? That seems so unlikely."

"To be here, you mean?" Birdie asked.

"Well, yes, to be here, but to exist at all. I thought Celtic language was primarily an oral tradition, not a language someone would have used in a printed book. I saw a show about it on TV."

"It's handwritten," Birdie said. "There are handwritten words in the beginning of the book."

"No ... there..." Ben began.

"Yes," Birdie said, cutting him off and opening her eyes wide, "there are."

"Nevertheless, I can just about guarantee you that the boy you said had this is not the owner," Mrs. Winggen said, closing the book and tucking it into her lap under a protective hand. "It's extremely old, for one thing, and very few people outside of Ireland know the language anymore. Even they are doing all they can to preserve it."

Birdie held a hand out in silent request.

"Would you like me to hold onto the book and see if I

can find the owners?" Mrs. Winggen asked.

"Thank you for offering," Birdie said more politely than she felt, "but we have some ideas about where to look next."

Mrs. Winggen loosened her grip on the volume reluctantly and handed it back to Birdie, looking all the while like she would have much preferred to slip it into the pocket of her coral sweater instead.

Birdie opened the cover again and studied the script, but it meant nothing to her. She turned the page. A new paragraph of the neat handwriting began in tiny letters at the very top edge of the thick paper and continued all the way to the bottom, carefully avoiding wasting any space. Birdie glanced at the next tightly written page, careful not to be rough with the brittle paper.

"I could take it back to the Benedictines at the Begijnhof for you," Mrs. Winggen offered. "The caretakers may have some idea where it came from. Yes, yes, that would be the place it most likely came from, since you found it at the Minnewater."

Birdie thought about the nun who was chasing the boy. Maybe she was chasing him for a good reason. Maybe he had stolen the book from the Begijnhof, not the bookstore.

"Now, now, don't look so glum," Mrs. Winggen said when neither Birdie nor Ben accepted her offer. "I'm sure you'll get to the bottom of this. How long will you be in Bruges?"

"One more day," Birdie said, eyeing the book doubtfully. She began to wrap it in the protective paper. "That doesn't give us much time."

"No, no it doesn't," Mrs. Winggen said. "But maybe you don't need much time. Time is a funny thing you know, it expands and contracts to suit itself. Some days seem to last forever and others fly by." She snapped her fingers. "Perhaps tomorrow will be one of those days."

They finished and thanked Mrs. Winggen for the tea.

"Oh, it was my pleasure," she said. "I always love a little company with my afternoon tea. And please bring that book back to me if you don't discover its owner before you leave. I'll see that it gets into the proper hands."

They left through the vestibule after another round of goodbyes during which Mrs. Winggen jotted her phone number on a slip of yellow paper and handed it to Birdie.

"Tuck that inside the book for safe keeping, so you know how to reach me if you don't finish your quest before you leave Bruges."

Ben and Birdie followed the narrow lane along the canal in silence until they reached the stone bridge.

"Hold up, Birdie," Ben said when they were halfway across.

"What is it?"

He'd stopped and was leaning against the stone wall that served as a railing. Behind him in the distance Mrs. Winggen's front door was shut tight once again. If it weren't for the pink and yellow flowers tumbling from the window boxes, it would appear as if no one lived there at all.

"The book changed," Ben said. He stared over the wall into the water that flowed slowly below them.

"I know."

"What do you think is going on?"

Birdie didn't respond.

Ben turned to face her.

Finally, she said, "I have no idea. None of this makes any sense at all. The book is ancient now. The pages are brittle. It's like it aged five hundred years in five minutes."

"Can I see it?"

Birdie sat on the wall and handed the package to Ben. He unwrapped it, opened the cover with extreme care, and tenderly turned the page.

The beautiful script was still there, taunting them with its curlicues and long elegant swoops, woven into letters and words that she didn't understand.

"A Traveler's Journal," Ben said.

"Maybe," Birdie said. "But we can't read it to be sure. Mrs. Winggen said it was in Celtic."

"It's not Celtic. I don't know why, but she was lying to us," Ben said. "That's what it says, right here," he pointed to the words. "*Journal D'Un Voyageur*. A Traveler's Journal. It's in French."

"French? How do you know?" she asked. She leaned over and examined the curlicues. She could make out a few letters, but was amazed that Mrs. Winggen could have been so wrong in her judgment. She was European, after all. Birdie would have thought she'd be more aware of the difference in languages.

"Yes," Ben said. "The script is old so it's hard to make out, but even I can recognize the words as French. I studied it a little in school."

"What else does it say?" she asked, turning the brittle paper to reveal the next page of tiny script.

Ben studied the page, moving the book closer to his face to get a better look. "Oh, Birdie, I'm not sure. I can make out words - it looks like something to do with the coast - *la côte* - but we would need to get help to translate it completely."

"We'd better be careful with it," Birdie said. "It seems so fragile now."

Ben gently turned another page. It was covered with the same tiny writing. It wasn't until they were one-quarter of the way through the book that they saw what had been there the night before - the first page of *The Game and Playe of the Chesse*.

"It's as if someone added pages, sewed them in somehow."

"I think that's exactly what happened," Ben said. "For

some reason someone wanted to use this book as a journal."

He closed the book and slipped it back into the pocket of his cargo shorts.

"So now what?" he asked.

"Let's go to Kayla's bookstore."

CHAPTER SIXTEEN

Books and Tea was tucked among a string of storefronts
along a curve of a lane in an area of Bruges that was more
residential than touristy. The buildings rose four skinny
stories with shops facing the street and apartments on the
upper floors. The buildings backed up to one of the many
canals, where double barn doors swung open to accept
deliveries by boat.

The front door of the small shop was painted the color of
a blue jay with two bejeweled stained-glass panels depicting
storybook scenes. They were smaller than the windows at
Mrs. Winggen's, but just as beautiful.

Birdie pushed on the heavy door and Ben followed her
inside.

Her nostrils flared at the heady aroma of old leather and
patchouli that greeted them as the door closed behind them,
winking out the bright day. Her eyes gradually adjusted to
the dim light and she studied the store.

"Whoa," Ben said.

On either side of them, narrow shelves crammed with all
manner of books climbed toward the towering ceiling,

where cobwebbed chandeliers hung dim and motionless. The shelves were filled with volumes of all shapes, sizes and thicknesses.

Birdie took a few steps down the center aisle of the store and stopped.

"I don't even know where to begin," she whispered.

Ben surveyed the space.

"There doesn't seem to be much logic in it," he said.

Indeed, there was no rhyme or reason to it at all. Birdie ran her hand across the uneven bindings of books in several languages, their names and topics and authors randomly stacked together.

"Looking for something in particular then?"

Birdie turned on her heel and found herself facing a bespectacled girl of about seventeen dressed in a black skirt and scarlet top, each cut to reveal a world of colorful tattoos on her lanky arms and legs. Her blond hair was clipped short except for one long lock that swung low across her right eye in a brilliant shade of blue. Her similarly colored eyes sparkled beneath the heavy black frames of her glasses. A handmade nametag fashioned from tiny crystals was pinned just below her collar. It read *Gretchen*.

"Oh, yes, we are, actually," Birdie said.

"Chess," Ben added, stepping up behind Birdie. "We're looking for books on chess."

"Ah ha!" Gretchen said, pushing her glasses up the bridge of her nose. "A popular topic here, to be sure." She waved her hand for them to follow her deeper into the store. "This way."

Ben and Birdie followed Gretchen through the towering stacks, skirting several piles of haphazardly arranged books on the wooden floor. They descended a dark set of stairs at the far end of the narrow shop, and exited in another part of the store where, unlike the jumble above, someone had taken a considerable amount of time and care to arrange books in various categories. At the far end of the room, wall-to-wall windows welcomed the sunlight and provided a lovely view of the sparkling canal beyond.

"Why is chess a popular topic here?" Birdie asked as they passed an orderly display of books related to Belgian chocolate making. The cover photos of luscious confections made her stomach rumble.

"Because of the books, of course," Gretchen replied. "You know, the first books?"

Ben and Birdie looked at her blankly.

Gretchen's colorful shoulders fell as she began to recite a story that Birdie could tell she had told many times before.

"In 1472, an Englishman named William Caxton became a partner in a printing shop in Bruges using technology he'd learned in Germany from Herr Gutenberg. He translated and printed the first ever book in English, right here, in Bruges. It was called *A Recuile of Histories of Troie*."

She pointed to a display featuring cutouts of Greek soldiers. They were pointing to tall stacks of neatly arranged leather-bound books. Several adults were standing around the table paging through them.

Ben and Birdie exchanged glances. That was the book Kayla said her grandparents had been so interested in.

"It was hugely popular, so he went on to translate and print a second book in English called *The Game and Playe of the Chesse*. That was the last book in English he ever printed here, as France, Belgium and England got themselves all mixed up in a conflict and he switched to printing in French and then by 1475 had uprooted himself and his press and moved to London."

"Did you say *The Game and Playe of the Chesse*?" Birdie asked, wanting to make absolutely sure she'd heard her correctly.

They skirted a table featuring a skull-and-crossbones

display of a book called *Bruges la Morte.*

Dead, Ben mouthed to Birdie, pointing a thumb back at the table.

"Yes, that's right," Gretchen said.

She continued leading them through the room, weaving past a variety of artfully arranged displays until they were in front of one with chess boards, figurines, and, as the foundation of it all, a stack of leather-bound books with a golden chess piece stamped on the front.

"It's not exactly a chess manual, even though that's what it sounds like," she said. "It's more of a moral guide, with examples of how people were supposed to behave using chess as an organizing principle."

Ben and Birdie exchanged glances.

"Yes, right. Here you are, then," Gretchen said. Before Ben and Birdie could thank her, she was making her way back through the room and up the stairs.

"Told you he stole it," Ben said, so only Birdie could hear.

"I'm not so sure, Ben." She studied the display. The golden knights on the covers sparkled in the sun coming through the tall windows.

"I am."

"Well, they look like our book, but they're not the same." She picked a copy up and handed it to Ben.

It was a fraction of the weight of the book he held in his pocket.

"Yeah, okay, I see what you mean. So then it's more likely he nipped it from the Begijnhof. I bet they have all kinds of old stuff there."

He opened the book. "It's just the chess book, only with simple black-and-white illustrations added. No handwriting."

"How much does it cost?"

Ben turned the book over and looked at the price sticker

on the back. "Wow. Twenty-five euros."

Birdie began to rummage in her daypack.

"What are you doing?" Ben asked.

"I think we should buy one."

"What? Why? That's a lot of money."

"I'd like to compare it to the one we have," Birdie said. "And the only other option is to steal it."

"Like the kid did."

"Exactly."

Ben dug deep into his cargo shorts and pulled out a few wrinkled bills and some coins. "Here's what I have."

"Thanks," Birdie said. She combined the two piles of cash on top of one of the chessboards and counted them out. "We should have enough to buy the book and still get something for lunch." She looked around the store. "Now where's Gretchen?"

With their new purchase in a paper bag that cost an extra euro and their old find securely in Ben's pocket, they made their way back outside.

"Let's try that place," Birdie said, pointing to a bright sandwich shop a few doors down on the quiet street. They ordered at the counter, and then found a shady table out front to wait for their lunch.

Ben shook his head and laughed as he settled his tall frame onto the tiny metal chair. "This is so weird."

"What?" Birdie asked.

"This place. This day. I mean, look around."

They were squeezed onto a slip of sidewalk on the narrow cobblestone lane, surrounded by ancient buildings, as if this was something they did every day.

"Not what you're used to?"

"Uh, no. Are you?"

"No," Birdie admitted. "This is nothing like home. The closest thing I've ever done was take a field trip to

Philadelphia. They have some narrow cobblestone streets, but it's not like this, a whole town preserved like it was the Middle Ages."

"See, there you go," he said. "Did you even know what the Middle Ages were before you came here?"

"Not really."

"I didn't. The closest I ever came was playing cloak-and-dagger video games."

Now it was Birdie's turn to laugh. "You're right. It's like a village in a video game."

"Do you play?" Ben's eyes brightened.

"Sometimes," Birdie said. "But not for a while."

This was true. The video game console that she'd once fought to get time on had sat dormant for more than a year, and was now packed up in a box deep in a storage unit across the Atlantic Ocean.

"I play all the time at home," Ben said. "I can disappear into my room and get away from my parents."

That sounded familiar. Jonah used to spend hours in the basement playing video games, although they were more likely to be sports games than cloak-and-dagger.

"Speaking of getting away from your parents, I'm totally amazed that my mom is letting me walk around without her," Birdie said. "It's definitely a first."

"Why? You're fifteen, right?"

"I turned fifteen in March, so not by much."

"She must think it's safe here."

"I guess," Birdie said. She looked up and down the lane. There was certainly nothing to be afraid of on this street in broad daylight. "But she's really careful at home. I'd never be allowed to walk around our town alone."

"Your mom said it's a college town, right?"

"Yes," Birdie said. "It has a different vibe than this place."

"Every place has a different vibe than this place. Besides,

it's not like either of us is wandering the streets by ourselves, we're together. And we're what? Four blocks from your mom?"

"That's true," Birdie said. And if she thought about it, she had been allowed to go off with Jonah sometimes, at the amusement park or even at the beach.

"So, where's your brother? Why didn't he come?" Ben asked, as if he were reading her thoughts.

A young woman with dark hair pulled into a messy bun delivered their sandwiches and two bags of chips - she called them crisps - on thin plates. Ben's was twice the size of Birdie's.

"I love these baguettes," he said, taking a large bite.

"The bread is good," Birdie agreed. "It's another thing that's not like home."

"Have you even seen a plain old piece of white bread here?"

"No," Birdie said. "But my mom never buys white bread at home, either."

"I love white bread. But I think I love this more." He took another giant bite of his sandwich.

When he finished chewing he asked Birdie about her brother again.

She took a deep breath.

"My brother died last year," she said. "With my dad." Her voice cracked but for once the tears stayed at bay. "They were in a bad car accident."

Ben stopped chewing and sat back in his chair.

"It's okay," Birdie continued. "We're okay. We're going to be okay. Everything is just ... different now."

"I'm sorry, Birdie," Ben said.

She saw the pain, the pity, in his eyes.

She knew that look. It was usually followed by horrible questions or some nervous excuse to get away from her, as if being too close would cause that person's family to die, too.

"Me, too," she said.

She picked at her sandwich.

Ben worked his way through his bag of chips in silence. Birdie figured he was trying to think of a polite way to pull the ripcord on the whole day.

Instead he said, "My parents are getting a divorce."

Now it was his turn to take a deep breath.

"They won't admit it to me, but I know what's going on. They basically hate each other. They used to fight all the time, but now they barely even talk to each other, which is worse if you ask me."

"I'm sorry, Ben," Birdie said. "That really stinks."

"Yeah, it does," Ben said. "They're pretty preoccupied with their problems. I got in trouble with some kids in town and they basically couldn't deal with it without screaming at each other so they sent me here with Uncle Noah. Out of sight, out of mind, right?"

"Have you talked to them at all?"

"Not really. Uncle Noah has sent them a couple of emails to let them know where we are, but that's about it."

"When do you go back to Texas?"

Ben let out a deep breath filled with what sounded like relief. "Not for a long time. We'll be in Europe until the end of August, assuming Uncle Noah and I don't kill each other first. He's dead serious about this brewery thing and he's trying to pack five years of education into a three month trip."

Two moms pushed strollers along the cobblestones and past the café, deep in conversation and oblivious to their babies' heads rattling along.

"What about you?" Ben asked. "How long are you staying?"

"We're spending the summer, too," Birdie said. She took a bite of her sandwich and finished chewing before she continued. "I'll go back in time for school to start in the fall.

We're hoping our house will be sold by then and we can move in somewhere new."

"You mean you don't know where you'll be living when you go home?"

"Nope, not yet anyway. Mom says we can always rent a place in town if the timing gets too tight. She doesn't want to pull me out of school."

"That makes sense."

"I thought so, too, but to be honest now that I'm here I'm not so sure. I'm not looking forward to going back."

"Why not?"

"Everything is different now," Birdie said. "Everyone is different."

Ben considered her for a moment.

"Well, we don't have to go back today," he said, clearing their empty plates to one side of the table. "Let's take a look at those books again."

CHAPTER SEVENTEEN

Ben gently tugged the book from his pocket as Birdie used her napkin to wipe the last of the crumbs onto the sidewalk. He set it on the table next to the plain paper bag that held the new version that Birdie bought.

"They are definitely not the same thing," Birdie said, pulling the new copy from the bag and lining it up next to the old one. They were close in size, but that was where the similarities ended.

"Most of the pages are copies," Ben said, flipping through the newer version. "They say the same thing and have the same illustrations, but you can tell they were printed using different methods. The new book is so clean and crisp. Look at the ink on the old book. It's bled into the page and made the letters fuzzy."

"It wasn't like that yesterday. I swear yesterday it was almost as crisp as the new one," Birdie said as she opened the fragile cover to reveal the first handwritten page. "Are you sure you don't know what the handwriting says on these front pages?"

Ben studied the tiny cursive. "I can tell that it's a journal, and I can make out some words here and there, but I'd really have to study it and maybe use a translator app to understand it. The writing is just so old."

"What if it disappears?" Birdie asked.

"The book?"

"Maybe, but no, I mean the journal pages. They weren't there when we first found the book, and then when we went to see Mrs. Winggen they showed up. What if the next time we look at the book they're gone again?"

"That seems unlikely."

"It seems unlikely that they're there at all," Birdie said.

"True."

Ben thought for a moment and then his eyes brightened. "You have a camera in your bag, don't you?"

"Yes, I do," Birdie said as she reached inside the patchwork sack and felt around for the camera. "That's a great idea."

She handed the camera to Ben. "No flash," she said.

"Shouldn't need it," he said, gesturing to the sunny day.

Birdie held each page open as Ben carefully lined them up in the camera's lens and snapped a picture. He checked each one to make sure it wasn't blurry.

"There," he said, handing the camera back to Birdie when he was sure all the photos were legible. "Now it doesn't matter if the pages disappear. We can still try to figure out what they say."

"And we shouldn't have to keep opening the book. I'm worried we'll damage it," Birdie said. "The corners of the pages feel like they want to snap off because they're so brittle. It was one thing when it seemed new, but now it's too fragile to keep messing with."

"Agreed."

Birdie looked at her watch. "You know, when we were on our way to Mrs. Winggen's house we passed by a sign for a library. We probably have just enough time to walk over there and see if we can use a computer."

"For what?"

"To see if we can translate some of what's on those pages."

Ben nodded appreciatively. "Not a bad idea."

"Hey, wait a minute," Birdie said a few minutes later when they turned down a deserted lane.

Ben stopped walking. "What?"

"I want to try something."

"What?"

"You see how narrow this lane is?"

"Yes."

Birdie looked up and down the street to make sure there were no cars or bicycles coming.

"Spread your arms as wide as you can."

"What?"

"Oh, just do it." Birdie stood a couple of feet away from him and spread her arms wide. Her fingertips just touched the stone facade of the house on the left side of the lane. Ben matched his fingertips to her outstretched right hand and reached for the crumbling red brick house on the opposite wall.

"Not quite," he said, stretching his lanky limbs.

"No," Birdie said, her grin wide. "But it sure is close!"

"You're crazy," Ben said, dropping his arms. "Now come on before we get creamed by a car."

They made their way back through the twisting lanes to one of the low stone bridges that spanned the water. They crossed over it and then took a seat on the canal wall.

Birdie pulled her mom's map out of her front pocket. "It was right around here somewhere. I remember seeing the sign."

Ben looked over her shoulder as she studied the map.

"There," he said, pointing to the words "*Bibliotheek*/Library" on the map. He glanced around to get his bearings.

"We should be able to walk down that lane over there," he said, "and then hang a right. We're close."

"Okay," Birdie said. She folded the map and put it back in her pocket. As she did, her fingers brushed against the piece of glass.

Birdie pulled out the aventurine so Ben could see it. She rubbed it. The knight held tight.

"It doesn't quite match anymore," Ben said. "The knight on the book is a mix of colors now."

"The gold probably faded with age. One thing's for sure, the knight on this glass doesn't want to budge," Birdie said. She rubbed it again and it grew warmer, but otherwise nothing happened.

"I guess it only had that one trick," Ben said. "To go from the flower to the knight."

"It was just so cool when it changed."

Ben sat back and crossed his arms behind his head. "That it was."

Birdie followed Ben's gaze up to the blue sky and then back to the row of medieval homes in front of them.

"Ben."

"What?"

"Do you see where we are?"

He looked around. "Sure, we're by Mrs. Winggen's..."

"Yes. Look at the flowers."

"Huh?"

"The flowers. In Mrs. Winggen's window box. They're red and purple again. Bright red and purple."

Ben lowered his arms and sat up straight on the wall.

"You're right. I didn't notice them when we sat down."

"Me neither. Let's go."

Birdie jumped off the wall and started down the narrow lane.

"Uh, Birdie, we can't bug that poor woman again," Ben said, jogging to catch up to her. "She's sure to tell Mrs. Devon and then Uncle Noah will find out."

"Just, come on."

A minute later they were standing in front of the red brick house.

"Look at those flowers," Birdie said.

"Yeah, they're great. Birdie..."

"Oh my gosh, there she is," Birdie whispered.

"Who?"

"The little girl. In the top window."

Ben took a step back and studied the top of the house. In the tallest window up under the eve a young girl stood looking down at them, her blond hair fanned in wide waves around her tiny face.

Birdie raised a hand and waved.

The girl waved back.

"Mrs. Winggen lied to us," Ben said.

"Yep."

"So, who's the girl?"

"No idea."

"Do you think she's a prisoner?" Ben asked. "That Mrs. Winggen is keeping her? Making her clean the house or something?"

"No idea."

"We should call the police, Birdie. We're lucky we got out of there alive."

A mew near their feet drew their attention from the window. An orange and yellow tabby cat wound through their legs, rubbing and purring.

"Go away, cat," Ben said, shooing it gently with his sneaker. He looked back at the window.

"She's gone," he said.

When Birdie looked up the little girl had stepped back into the room.

"She's still there," Birdie said. "I can just make out her shadow."

A whistle sounded at the end of the block and the cat slinked away toward it. Birdie followed its silky movement and discovered the source of the whistle.

"That's him," Birdie said. She took a step forward.

Ben touched her shoulder. "Careful. Let's not scare him away again."

"He doesn't look scared," she said as she slipped the warm aventurine back into her front pocket.

In fact, he was jogging toward them, sort of shimmering as he approached.

"*Mon livre*," he called as soon as he was close enough for them to hear. He continued forward until he stood right in front of them.

He was about the same height as Birdie, which meant Ben towered over both of them. The boy's eyes were green with flecks of pale blue, framed by sandy blond hair falling in loose waves across his forehead and nearly brushing his shoulders.

This close she realized that he was just her age. She'd thought he was younger, but now she realized he was not.

"I'm sorry. I don't understand. Do you speak English?" Birdie asked.

"His book," Ben began.

But the boy nodded. "*Un peu. Mon livre, s'il vous plait.*" He paused and carefully formed the words. "A little. My book ... please."

His voice was thick with accent and he spoke like someone who knew only a few words of English.

He was dressed in the same odd attire she'd seen him in before, except he'd added plain leather shoes that looked a bit like moccasin boots, only without the fringes. Like his pants, the shoes sagged as if they were too big.

"How do we know it's yours?" Ben asked.

"How do you know we have it?" Birdie asked, speaking as slowly and clearly as she could.

The boy took a moment to process the words. Then he said, "*Je vous vois dans le parc.* I saw you in the park."

The French didn't help Birdie at all.

Then Ben said, "*Oui, nous trouvons le livre dans le parc. C'est votre?*"

"What did you just ask him?" Birdie asked, staring at Ben in complete surprise. "And I thought you said you didn't know French?"

He grinned. "I told him we found the book in the park and asked if it's his."

"*Oui,*" the boy replied, nodding vigorously. "*Je cache le livre. C'est mienne.*"

"He says he hid it in the park and it's his."

Birdie didn't know if she was more surprised by Ben or the boy.

The boy held out his hand.

"Ask him what his name is."

"My name," the boy said slowly, clearly proud that he'd understood Birdie's question, "is Henri."

"*Bonjour,* Henri," Birdie said, repeating the name as he'd said it so it sounded like On-Ree. She was grateful that she at least knew how to say hello in French. "My name is Birdie and this is Ben."

Henri looked at Ben. He held out his hand. "*Mon livre,* Ben, *s'il vous plait.*"

Ben pulled open the flap of his shorts pocket and reached inside for the book.

"Birdie, look," he said as he pulled it out and unwrapped the paper.

The knight on the cover was bright gold again and the book looked old but new.

Before Birdie could respond, a high-pitched horn blasted behind them in the narrow lane.

Ben and Birdie jumped up onto the sliver of curb along the canal wall. They flattened themselves against it as a BMW zoomed past.

"Maniac!" Birdie yelled after it.

They stepped back down onto the cobblestones.

"Where did he go?" Ben asked, turning in a circle in the middle of the lane.

"What?" Birdie said.

"Henri. Damn it! He's gone again."

Birdie spun around on the spot. There were a few wayward tourists, but there was no sign of the boy.

"Henri!" she called into the crowd. A few people looked at her curiously but there was no sign of him.

"Don't bother, Birdie. He's gone," Ben said.

He pointed to the house in front of them.

The flowers had faded back to pink and yellow.

CHAPTER EIGHTEEN

"So, you can't read French, huh?" Birdie said as they made their way back to the bed and breakfast, the trip to the library forgotten in the excitement of meeting Henri.

Ben laughed. "Well, I couldn't read the French in that book. Did you see how old it was? It was like reading Middle English."

"Well you sure spoke to Henri with no problem."

"I know a little," Ben said.

"Where did you learn it?"

"Oh, when I was little my parents sent me to this special preschool and one of the things they taught us was a foreign language. I was in the section of kids that learned some French. It stuck in my brain okay. Last year they started offering it in school so I got a refresher. I did pretty well so I started practicing online on my own. Did you know there are free language apps? I don't know that much, but I can get by with basic words. I've been trying to learn at least the basics for every country we're visiting."

"You sounded like you knew enough to me. My school doesn't even offer French," Birdie said. "It's Spanish or nothing."

"Our school is pretty big," Ben said. "So there are lots of choices. But not many kids take French. There were only about ten students in my class. All girls except for me. The school will probably drop it at some point."

"Well, I'm glad they didn't drop it yet," Birdie said.

"Yeah, me, too."

"We're going to need to figure out some way to get that book to Henri," Birdie said. "This is getting nuts."

"I know and I can't stop thinking about that little girl. What was she doing up in the room?"

"Maybe I should tell my mom about her."

"Do you think she would believe you?"

"I don't know. And I can't be sure she'd be around even if my mom did believe me and we went back to Mrs. Winggen's house."

"Maybe we could sneak through her back door or something."

"I don't know, Ben."

"Well, do you have any better ideas?"

Birdie thought for a moment. "Not right now," she said. "But give me some time to think about it. Maybe I'll come up with something."

Ben nodded. "Better make it quick, though. Time is something we're short on."

When they arrived at the bed and breakfast it was nearly time for Uncle Noah to return.

"I'm going to go see if my mom is back," Birdie said.

"Do you want the book?"

"No, you can hold onto it. I can't read it anyway."

"Maybe I can use Uncle Noah's computer to try to translate those handwritten pages. We're supposed to go to some special place called the Monk Bar tonight for dinner. Maybe he'll let me out of it."

Birdie shrugged. "Okay, but I doubt it since you spent the day with us. Let me know if you find anything out." She reached into the pocket of her jeans and pulled out the piece of glass. "Here. Hold onto this, too. Maybe the handwriting says something about it."

"Are you sure?" He eyed the aventurine.

"I'm sure. You can give it back to me tomorrow before we leave."

Ben turned the cool piece of glass over in his palm.

"Still the knight," he said.

Birdie nodded. "Okay, see you tomorrow," she said.

Ben unlocked the door to the room he shared with Uncle Noah on the first landing. Birdie continued up the final flight of stairs to the attic.

"There you are," Mrs. Blessing said when Birdie came into the sunny room and kicked off her sneakers. "I was beginning to think I was going to need to call in the search party."

"Sorry. Have you been here long?"

"No. I got back about ten minutes ago."

"How was lace-making?"

"Hard," Mrs. Blessing admitted. "But I made this."

She held up a piece of white lace about the size of a coffee coaster. The fabric wove together to form a flower.

"It's pretty," Birdie said. "You made it?"

"I did. It took me all afternoon. You should see the older women who do this, Birdie. They move so fast. Their hands are like little machines. For every one loop I made they made at least seven or eight."

"Wow," Birdie said.

"I got some sketching done, too, just a little bit during the breaks." She showed Birdie a design she was working on for a wall hanging that resembled the arched windows of a church. She was finally getting the hang of the stained glass. The drawing reminded Birdie of the lion and the bear in the door in Mrs. Winggen's vestibule.

"It looks great," Birdie said. Her mom seemed to come alive again when she was working on her designs. It was the only time that the shadows seemed to completely lift around her.

"So, what's on the agenda for tonight?" Birdie asked.

"Not much. I figured we'd find a little bistro for dinner and then come back here. I'd like to get some more work done."

"Sounds good to me."

Actually, it sounded great. She flopped down on the edge of the bed.

"How was your day with Ben?"

"Good," Birdie said. "The bookstore was neat."

Mrs. Blessing nodded, but Birdie could tell she had refocused on her sketch. Birdie settled back against her bed pillow.

"Oh, and I decided to leave a little later tomorrow instead of first thing in the morning," Mrs. Blessing said. "I want to go back to the church to see the Michelangelo statue again. We were so tired when we were there the first time and they were closing up. I'm not sure I really gave it the attention it deserved. We're driving so we have some flexibility about when we leave."

Birdie nodded. "We're going to Germany?"

"Yes. To the Rhine and Mosel Rivers. There are some old castles there I want to check out."

"Castles, really?"

Mrs. Blessing looked up again and smiled at her daughter. "Really."

"Cool," Birdie said.

Bruges is generally safe,
even on the back lanes
late at night.

Marty McEntire's
Europe for Americans Travel Guide

CHAPTER NINETEEN

Birdie tossed the warm duvet off her legs and swung them over the side of the bed.

The room was dark except for a patch of moonlight that fell over her bed from the open attic window.

A sound like gravel kicking up behind a truck tire came from beneath the windowsill. She'd been listening to the noise in her dreams for what seemed like hours, hitting the white stone and scattering again and again.

Across the room Mrs. Blessing's breathing was steady and smooth.

Birdie dropped her bare feet onto the cool wooden planks and slipped silently from the bed.

The noise rose again.

Her heart raced as she stepped to the window on soft feet and peered outside. She expected to see gravel on the windowsill, but it was bare.

The street below was dark except for the moonlight that danced across the cobblestones. The wind blew the dark clouds across the sky, an undulating mass of grey and black slipping over and past the moon.

Flowers fluttered in the window boxes along the narrow street.

An errant sheet of newspaper lifted and dipped in the air, following the current toward the arched intersection.

It felt like ages since she'd slipped under that arch with her mom, so worried about beating the clock to reach the keypad before the code changed.

A rush of cold air passed over her warm skin.

She shivered.

The street was deserted.

She listened, waiting.

Nothing.

Had she imagined the noise? Had it been in her dream after all?

She glanced at the clock on the nightstand.

Half past two.

This is ridiculous, she thought, turning back to the window for one final inspection of the narrow lane below.

Birdie gasped, then covered her mouth to silence herself.

Her mother's breath continued steadily behind her.

Three stories below, Henri and the little girl were standing near the corner where the alley flowed into the lane.

The tabby cat sat properly by the girl's feet, which were barely visible beneath her long dress.

They were staring up at her window, almost shimmering in the moonlight.

Birdie lifted her hand in acknowledgement.

When she did, Henri did not wave back, but gestured for her to come down to the street. As he did a gust of wind whistled through, stirring leaves from the window boxes into a whirlwind that flew skyward in tight formation until the air it rode on stopped. The dead leaves hung suspended for a moment before drifting down to the cobblestones.

Henri motioned to her again.

This was crazy. She did not want to be out after dark.

She checked the windows of the surrounding houses but the shutters and curtains were all drawn tight. The only shadows were the long ones thrown by Henri, the girl, and the cat as they stood in the moonlight waiting for her.

No.

She was not going downstairs.

She was not going outside in the middle of the night.

She backed away from the window and sat down on the edge of her bed.

Her heart thundered.

Gravel hit the stone beneath the windowsill.

She closed her eyes and willed Henri and the little girl to go away.

Gravel scattered again.

No.

She'd never get past her mother and even if she did she'd be in such trouble if she got caught.

And what if she did go down there and it was all for nothing?

What if she got down there and Henri had disappeared again?

He had a bad habit of disappearing.

She stepped back to the window. They were still there, waiting.

Henri gestured to her again, more urgently.

Birdie hesitated.

But then, what if Ben was right and the little girl was being held by Mrs. Winggen and Henri had rescued her?

What if he'd brought her here so Birdie could take her in and call the police?

What if Birdie was the little girl's only hope?

She looked down at her, so small in the dark night. She must be terrified.

She had to do something.

Should she wake up her mom?

She watched her sleeping for a moment.

No.

This was probably a wild goose chase and she wasn't going to disturb her mom when she was finally sleeping soundly.

Birdie picked up her jeans and jacket from the floor beside the bed where she'd dropped them when she changed into her pajamas. Her hands shook as she slid them on.

She thought for sure her heartbeat was audible in the quiet night.

She tiptoed across the room, willing herself to be as light and invisible as possible.

Mrs. Blessing shifted in the bed and her breath changed rhythm.

Birdie froze mid-step.

She closed her eyes.

If she got caught now she could just say she was going to the bathroom.

Right.

The bathroom.

She opened her eyes.

From the open window a noise floated into the room. It sounded like a horse and carriage rattling past.

Birdie moved swiftly around the corner to the bedroom door, her movement disguised by the sound outside.

She picked up her sneakers and paused, listening.

Her mother's breath was steady again.

She turned the key ever so slowly in the lock, one full twist, and then, Click!

It unlocked and popped open an inch. She pulled it open as quietly as possible, just far enough to slip through.

A moment later she was in the dark hallway, the bedroom door closed behind her. She let out her breath.

She located the small white dot on the ceiling that activated the motion sensor. It was at the far end of the stairwell. She flattened herself against the wall and walked sideways down the steps to avoid triggering it.

She moved at a snail's pace, attempting to limit the amount of stair creaking and avoid the motion sensors.

She rounded the corner and slid past the door to Ben's room undetected.

She wanted to wake him more than anything, but there was no way to manage it without knocking on his door and waking the rest of the house - and Uncle Noah - at the same time.

She took several deep breaths.

She was convinced she would never make it all the way down to the foyer.

But she did.

Almost.

She stood pinned against the mirrored wall two steps above the mosaic floor, her sneakers dangling from her left hand.

She studied the dark foyer.

She determined that there was no way to reach the front door and open it without tripping the light sensor.

She took a deep breath and barreled across the tiny tiles, shielding her eyes against the bright light of the chandelier.

She opened the heavy door as quickly and quietly as she could and then slipped outside.

She collapsed on the front stoop, her heart hammering against her ribs and her legs shaking.

She closed her eyes again and took a few more deep, steady breaths.

They sounded ragged, but she knew that was normal. The grief counselor had taught her how to breathe to fight the panic attacks that plagued her in the first months after Jonah and her dad died. She whispered the mantra she'd been taught, taking a deep breath between each sentence:

"I am in no danger here."

"I am in no danger here."

"I am in no danger here."

She never imagined she'd be using her counselor's advice to sneak out of the house.

She bet the counselor never imagined it, either.

The breathing technique was beginning to work.

"I am in no danger here."

When she felt her heartbeat return to nearly normal she opened her eyes. They had adjusted to the darkness and she could easily see in the moonlit night.

She cranked her sneakers on without bothering to untie them, then stood on calm legs and examined the deserted street. As she did another gust of wind flared though it.

Birdie pulled her jacket tighter and zipped it up.

There was no sign of Henri, or the little girl, or even the tabby cat.

"Really?" she said to herself. "Where are you guys?"

Across the street a curtain shifted in a second-story window. Birdie caught the movement from the corner of her eye but didn't look up.

She had to make a decision.

She couldn't stay mounted on the stoop like a potted plant forever.

This is not smart, she thought, but pushed it from her brain.

She was already out here and would be in big trouble if she got caught. She might as well see if she could figure out what Henri wanted. Maybe he'd left a clue in the alley. Maybe she could help.

She tucked her hands in her jacket pockets, bowed her head and stepped off the stoop, watching her footing on the uneven cobbles. She avoided looking at the houses that lined the narrow lane. She did not want to see if anything lurked there, waiting behind the drawn curtains and shuttered windows.

She crossed the lane and turned into the dark alley where the children and the cat had stood.

She had no idea how much time had passed since she'd waved to them from the window.

One thing was for sure: there was no sign of them now.

She examined the cobblestones beneath her feet and searched for anything the children may have left behind.

Her eye caught on a small shiny object a few inches away.

As she bent to retrieve it, a strong hand gripped her right arm above the elbow.

She was so startled that she barely had time to process what was happening before stifling the scream that bubbled in her throat.

CHAPTER TWENTY

"Birdie, shush. It's me."

Ben.

She twisted in his grasp, using her free hand to push him hard in the chest. "You scared me half to death!"

He didn't move but his angular face brightened with surprise.

"Ah, come on, Birdie. I wasn't going to let you come out here alone. Besides, I thought you had something against sneaking out."

"I ... Henri..." she began. She tried to motion down the alley but Ben still had hold of her arm.

"Yeah. I saw them, too," he said, dropping his hand now that he could be sure Birdie wouldn't scream and wake up the neighborhood. "No sign of them now, though."

"Did you bring the book?" Birdie asked as she searched the street around them for any sign of the other children. She tried to pick up the shiny object but realized it was just a marking on a cobblestone.

Ben patted the pocket of his camouflage shorts drawing Birdie's attention back to him.

"How many pairs of cargo shorts do you own?" she asked.

Ben smiled his crooked smile. "Is there any other kind?"

"Oh, here," he said, pulling the aventurine from the back pocket of his shorts and handing it to her. "Before I forget. We ended up going to that Monk Bar so I hardly had any time to use the computer. I was trying to find something out about the knight when I heard Henri throwing rocks at the windows."

"Thanks," Birdie said as he dropped the aventurine on her palm. It felt warm. "Okay, so what are we going to do? We need a plan."

"Well, we're out here now. If we get caught we're going to be in deep sh..."

"Yeah, I know."

"So we might as well make it worthwhile."

Ben started down the alley. Birdie fell into step beside him.

"Where are you going?" Birdie asked him.

"Not sure."

They came to the bend in the canal.

Henri was there crouched against the wall with the little girl tucked up behind him.

"Oh, thank God," Birdie whispered.

As they drew closer, Birdie smiled at the little girl. She was wearing a long dress and her wavy blond hair fell into green eyes that looked like Henri's.

"I have the book," Ben said. The Velcro flap on his shorts pocket produced a ripping noise as he opened it. "*J'ai la livre.*"

Henri nodded and held out his hand in silent request.

"It's strange, " Ben began, as he carefully pulled the volume free from the fabric. "The book changed..."

A growling noise rose up behind them.

Birdie's heart rose to her throat as she whirled around,

expecting to see a wild dog snarling there.

What she saw instead made it nearly stop beating altogether.

A shimmering pack of boys was making its way up the alley. They carried small bats and large rocks.

"LeFort!" a tall one called menacingly. As he drew closer Birdie could see that his nose looked like it had been broken and poorly reset more than once.

"*Au sucor*," Henri whispered to Ben, his eyes pleading. Then he turned to the little girl. "*Cours, Mary! Cours!*"

Henri and Mary sprinted up the alley, banking in opposite directions at an intersection several yards away.

Ben grabbed Birdie's arm and pulled her up onto the stoop of one of the houses that lined the alley. They ducked behind a pair of lion statues that guarded the front door.

The boys rumbled past at full speed, yelling and cursing as if Ben and Birdie weren't even there.

"It's like they didn't even see us," Birdie said.

"Come on!" Ben said, jumping from the stoop and chasing after the boys as they turned down the path Henri had taken.

"What did Henri say to you?" Birdie cried, breathing hard as they ran at full speed.

"Help," Ben said. "He asked for help."

Birdie ran harder.

They reached the end of the lane, turned right onto a main street and then banked left into another alley, chasing the sound of the boys' soft-soled shoes as they slapped against the cobblestones. The alley circled back to the canal where the slow-moving water reflected the moon as it slipped in and out of the clouds, creating a surreal nightlight along the misty water.

They tucked in close to the stone wall that traced the canal, the bulky figures of the boys just visible far ahead in the dark.

"I hope he loses them," Birdie said, her breath coming in quick bursts.

"Me, too."

"Those boys," she said, "they're trouble."

Ben and Birdie crept along the wall as quickly and quietly as they could. They didn't want to draw the attention of the boys. They had ignored them once. They might not be so lucky a second time.

The houses that lined the other side of the canal opened up into a dark expanse. It was familiar to Birdie, and she realized they were near the park and the brewery where they had first seen Henri.

"There," Ben said, pointing to a low stone bridge.

They crossed it, staying down, and slipped into the Minnewater. They passed the tree where Henri had hidden the book and followed a path of crushed grass through the gate leading into the Begijnhof.

On the other side of the gate, a church rose high above the overgrown courtyard and windswept trees cast shadows across the moonlit ground. Whitewashed brick bungalows bordered the courtyard on every side.

They stopped and listened for the boys, but the courtyard was silent.

Birdie wished she'd never left the safety of her warm bed. Henri wasn't here, and neither was Mary or even those boys.

She touched Ben's shoulder.

"Maybe we should turn back," she said, her voice low.

Ben pointed to the tall grass in front of them. "They're still here. Look how this grass is trampled."

A path cut through the courtyard to another gate on the far end.

"What if we find them? If we catch up? What then?" Birdie asked.

"We'll make sure Henri and Mary are okay."

"But..."

Ben whirled around and faced Birdie. She took a half a step back in surprise.

"But what?"

She looked into his eyes. Jonah had confronted her just like this a million times. She'd always felt so small and stupid when he did. The words would never come.

But Ben wasn't looking at her like she was stupid. He was exasperated, to be sure, but not angry.

"Look, Birdie," he said, spreading his hands wide. "I know you're scared. I'm a little freaked out, too. But we started this and I think we should finish it."

"Return the book."

"Yes."

"And then we can go back to the bed and breakfast."

"And back to our normal, ordinary, safe, lives."

Birdie took a deep breath.

Ben waited.

Finally she nodded, then stepped forward to lead the way across the grass to the far gate.

They passed through it and into a clearing awash in moonlight. Benches and well-groomed hedges lined the circular space and a fountain pulsed in the center. Two women made of stone stood forever watching the flow of the water. A white cottage with darkened windows stood sentinel on the far side of the clearing.

The group of ill-intentioned boys milled around in front of it.

A flash of movement to the right of the cottage caught Birdie's attention. She barely made out Henri's shadow as he pushed Mary through a passage in the hedge and then slipped through behind her.

"Ben," she began but the words died in her throat as one of the boys called to his mates using words that Birdie didn't understand but a tone that she couldn't mistake.

Henri was in big trouble.

The boys barreled through the passage, pushing and shoving each other as they cleared the hedge.

"Let's go." Ben sprinted across the clearing with Birdie at his heels.

They ducked through the hedge, their nostrils filling with the scent of pine needles. When they came out on the other side, Birdie's shoulders were damp with dew.

She shivered.

They were on a dirt path that snaked along another canal, this one smaller than the last, past an imposing brick building supported by a series of Gothic arches.

Henri and Mary were darting down the path. If they looked back they'd see the boys gaining on them.

Birdie held her breath. She almost couldn't watch. There was no way they could outrun those boys.

Ben started down the path and Birdie followed. As they did, Henri grabbed Mary by the arm and pulled her under one of the building's stone arches. Their figures faded to black, as if they'd disappeared.

The boys pulled up short and scattered.

Ben and Birdie watched them run away.

"That was weird," Birdie said.

"They didn't want to follow Henri in there, that's for sure," Ben said.

"I wonder why?"

"Let's go find out."

"Are you serious?"

"If Henri took Mary in there it can't be that bad."

Birdie wasn't so sure, but she took a deep breath and followed Ben. One thing she did know was that she did not want to be out here by herself if those boys came back.

They reached the building and passed under the archway where Henri and Mary had been only moments before. In front of them, stone stairs corkscrewed down into blackness.

Birdie and Ben felt their way forward on the stairs until they reached the bottom.

There was a door.

Birdie pushed it open.

A low murmuring stopped as Ben followed Birdie across the threshold, where they stood rooted to the spot.

In the Middle Ages, many children
left home at about age ten for education
or to go to work as servants. Those who
didn't have a father were assigned another
male relative to oversee their upbringing, or,
if there were no other male relatives,
given to a male member of the
community that the Aldermen
found acceptable.

Marty McEntire's
Europe for Americans Travel Guide

CHAPTER TWENTY-ONE

The room before them was like nothing Birdie had ever seen before.

At first it felt like a dank, dark basement in a very old house, one where the floor was made of dirt. But it was like no other basement she'd ever been in. Low stone arches marched overhead, forming hidden alcoves behind the thick pillars that supported them. It reminded Birdie of the Jerusalem Church, only without a soaring steeple to let in light. The only light, in fact, flickered from candles deep within the alcoves.

It smelled terrible. The air was thick with mildew, smoke, the scent of well-cooked sausages, and something else that Birdie didn't want to identify.

Henri stepped out from the shadows of the alcove closest to the door. He gripped Birdie's wrist with surprising strength and she nearly dropped the aventurine she'd been holding. She passed it to her other hand and slipped it into the pocket of her jeans.

Henri held tight to her wrist as he pulled her deeper into the long chamber. Ben followed close behind them, ducking his head under each low arch. When one of Birdie's sneakers caught on the roughly cobbled floor, he leaned in to steady her.

"This is the Monk Bar," he whispered.

She nodded but thought she could not have heard him correctly.

This was no bar. There were no stools for one thing, and no heavy wooden tables like she'd seen at the café the other night. The floor was a disaster of uneven stones that even a sober person would struggle to navigate.

A weak campfire burned near the center of the dim corridor, its gray smoke floating to the ceiling where it hugged the stone arches before dissipating. Several boys sat at a table near it, bent over a game of dice. They looked up as Ben, Birdie, and Henri approached.

The beefiest of the group, a young man whom the others called Jan and whose face resembled a deflated beach ball, sneered when he saw Henri. He used his elbow to get the attention of the kid sitting next to him, who looked up with hunched over features that reminded Birdie more of a rat than a boy of about fifteen.

"LeFort, the witch's daughter is coming," the boy sneered. "She will torture you while you sleep."

Henri ignored them and they all laughed.

"Do not look at them," Henri murmured so only Birdie could hear.

She did as he instructed, and instead peered into each alcove they passed.

The Gothic arches hid the faces of dozens of children who appeared to live there amid piles of clothing, blankets and broken things.

She hesitated when they reached an alcove of sleeping children, so thin and small that they appeared as piles of dirty rags rather than little humans.

Henri jerked her hard to the right and she stumbled,

catching herself only when firm hands grabbed her upper arms.

Birdie lifted her head and found herself staring into the dull blue eyes of a girl who stood only slightly taller than she did. She was extremely thin, but also quite strong judging by the pain in Birdie's arms from her grip.

"*Anglais,*" Henri said.

The girl nodded and dropped her hands from Birdie's arms. Henri released her wrist.

Birdie shook her arm out and then rubbed the spot on her wrist where his finger marks remained.

"Welcome," the girl said, her voice low and raspy in the smoky room.

"Who are you?" Ben demanded, stepping forward so he stood beside Birdie. "What's going on here?"

"Henri, you may leave us," she said.

Henri bowed his head slightly and stepped away.

The older girl's long straight hair hung nearly to her waist. It was the color of straw and partially tucked into a hat that reminded Birdie of a throw pillow. It looked as if it had been a long time since it had been washed. She was dressed as oddly as Henri, in thick leggings and a dark overcoat that dwarfed her slender form.

The candlelight revealed a modest space behind her that was orderly and decorated in a way that the other alcoves hadn't been. Thickly woven, frayed tapestries hung against each of the three walls. On the far end, a tattered duvet covered a bed made of wooden crates. On the other side, a large wooden barrel served as a desk and a smaller one as a makeshift chair.

The candles threw a brighter light here, their thickness and quantity superior to those in the rest of the dungeon.

The dungeon, Birdie thought with a start. She was in a dungeon with strange kids from Bruges. Did they do this often? Lure stupid tourists to their lair in the middle of the night and then do God knows what to them? What had she been thinking?

"My name is Eva."

Birdie remained silent, scanning the room for something she could use as a weapon. Her options were limited: a candlestick, a wooden barrel, a spool of twine.

She was glad for Ben standing beside her. They didn't speak but she would have bet money he was also trying to figure the best way out of this mess.

It was a long way back to the door they entered, but maybe there was a back door somewhere.

"Do you have a name?" the girl asked, bringing Birdie's attention back to her.

"My name is Birdie." She was grateful that her voice didn't quiver.

Eva threw her head back and laughed. The low sound echoed through the dark corridor and chilled Birdie to the bone.

"And you?" she asked, sizing Ben up. She cocked her head at his bare knees. "Is your name Fox?"

She laughed again, clearly amused at her own joke.

"We need to get back," Birdie said.

"Eva," Ben said evenly. "My name is Benjamin."

"Ah, he can speak," Eva said, meeting his eyes. "A proper Christian name, too, I see. But what has happened to your pants?"

Eva had stopped laughing but a glint of humor remained in her eyes. "And you, my little swallow, where is your gown?"

Her questions were met with silence. Even the children in the alcoves were quiet. Birdie imagined they were listening, waiting for a sign to know if she and Ben were friend or foe.

"Ah yes," Eva continued when they didn't respond.

"Benjamin and Birdie. Aren't you curious why Henri brought you here?"

Neither Birdie nor Ben said anything, but Birdie's mind raced. Had Henri led them here on purpose? Had this been his plan all along, to bring them to this dank place? They would be sorely disappointed if they tried to rob them. They'd spent their money on lunch and the new chess book earlier that day. Had it only been that day? The only thing in Birdie's pocket now was the aventurine.

She almost slid her hand into her pocket to grasp it, to protect it, but she caught herself just in time. Such a move would alert everyone that there was something of value there. She held still but each nerve in her body sprang to attention.

"I asked," Eva said, moving closer to Birdie, "because I am curious about you." She focused on Birdie. "Henri says you appeared one day on the brewery roof. You just, appeared."

She opened her hand as if she were tossing pixie dust into the air. "And then you," she raised her eyes to take in Ben's tall frame. "You appeared, too."

The three of them stood silently in the dim candlelight.

"You have nothing to say?" Eva asked.

"We're on vacation," Birdie shrugged, as if this was the most natural exchange she'd ever had.

"Vacation?" Eva repeated. She rolled the word around in her mouth.

"Yes. We're on ... holiday," Birdie said. "We're American."

Eva threw her head back and laughed again.

Birdie didn't like being laughed at. "And why are you here?" she asked. "Hiding out?"

Eva's laugh turned into something more like a snarl. "We must hide, you fool. We are not free to walk around like you."

"Why not?" Ben asked.

Eva met his eyes, startled as if she'd momentarily forgotten he was there. "If we are seen we will be taken before the Aldermen, and if we are lucky, put with a family that will work us to death. If we are not lucky, we will be sent back from whence we came."

"From whence you came? And where exactly did you come from? Why are you really here? Are you all runaways? Where are your parents?" Birdie thought for a moment. She dropped her voice low. "Or is someone holding you here?"

Adrenaline surged through her. She dared a hard look at Ben. He was surveying the room, clearly looking for the best escape. They had to get out of here and fast.

"We all choose to be here," Eva said, dismissing the suggestion of being captive. "It is our last choice. Our parents are dead. The plague left us at the mercy of distant family. This city is dying, too. The port is full of silt. The foreign ships no longer come. The guilds and the merchants fight in the streets. Those who did not succumb to the plague are leaving, abandoning the city, abandoning us. Only those with no options left have stayed."

"Then what do y'all want from us?" Ben asked.

"The book. It does not belong to you," Eva said. "Henri says you have his book."

"The chess book?" Ben asked. "Maybe we do and maybe we don't. Why is it so important?"

"It is ours. That is all you need to know." She did not meet Ben's eyes when she spoke, but stared coldly into Birdie's.

"Well, I don't have it right now," Birdie said, only half-lying. It was in Ben's pocket, not hers. "Not with me anyway."

There was no way she was giving Henri's book to this girl. She didn't know what was going on, but she was fairly certain that Henri wouldn't have led them here if that gang of boys hadn't been on his tail. And now he was nowhere to be found.

"Bring it to me," Eva said. "And Henri and Mary will continue to have our protection."

"We found the book in the park," Birdie said. "What right do you have to it?"

"It belonged to Henri's father," Eva said.

"Henri's father?" Ben asked. "What happened to his parents?"

"Have you not been listening? The sickness took them. It spared Henri and Mary but only them."

"Why was Henri running from the old woman?" Birdie asked.

"Old woman?"

"The one at the park."

"Park?"

"Um, the Minnewater? A nun maybe?"

"Ah. The Beguine," Eva said. "She thinks the book belongs to her, but she could not use it anyway."

"And you can use it?" Ben asked.

"Of course."

"For what?" Birdie asked.

Eva ignored the question. "You will bring it here. Tomorrow night."

Birdie nodded. Tomorrow night was perfect. She'd be well on her way to Germany by then.

One thing was for sure at the moment, however, that leather-bound book was their ticket out of this place.

"Tomorrow," she said. "We'll bring it back to the park and leave it where we found it."

Eva nodded, then looked beyond Birdie's shoulder.

"Henri?" she called.

He skittered forward.

"We are done here."

Henri nodded, then motioned for Ben and Birdie to

follow him. As they passed one of the alcoves, Henri ducked inside and picked up Mary, who had snuggled in with several other children on a pile of rags.

"Henri!" Eva called.

"*Oui?*"

"You will stay."

He nodded, then led Ben and Birdie through the wooden door and back up the spiral stairs to the dirt path. To Birdie's great relief there was no sign of the boys who'd been chasing Henri and Mary earlier.

"*Le livre,*" Henri whispered. "It belongs to me."

Then he turned and, carrying his small sister in his arms, disappeared back into the stairwell, leaving Ben and Birdie alone on the path.

The sky cleared momentarily and the moon lit the way to the hedge.

They ran.

CHAPTER TWENTY-TWO

"You did what?" Kayla demanded.

"Keep your voice down," Ben said.

Birdie had never seen Kayla show any emotion other than boredom, and certainly not anger. Before now Birdie would have said Kayla didn't care enough about anything or anyone to be angry.

Except maybe her phone.

"You could've been kidnapped or killed, you idiots."

"We were fine," Ben said. "And keep your voice down before you wake up the whole house."

"You should have told me you were going."

They were in a small bedroom on the second floor of t'Bruges Huis, two doors down from the room Ben shared with his uncle. It held one twin bed covered by a yellow duvet like the one in Birdie's room, a desk, a small night stand, and, from what Birdie could tell, a tiny bathroom behind a flowered curtain that hung half open. Kayla had scared them half to death when she cracked her door open and ushered them inside as they made their way back up the stairs.

Now Ben stood leaning against the wall with his long legs crossed at the ankles and his arms crossed against his chest. Birdie sat in the chair at the desk.

"Why would we tell you?" Ben replied. "You couldn't have cared less what Birdie and I have been doing."

"Maybe if we'd made a YouTube video about it," Birdie said under her breath. Ben's mouth twisted but he was too irritated with Kayla to laugh.

And when it came right down to it, they were both too relieved to be back at the bed and breakfast to care much about getting waylaid by Kayla.

"Well, I didn't know you were going to end up sneaking out," Kayla said, slumping back onto her bed. Birdie saw a pout flirt with her lips but then she recovered. "You should have told me so I could have gone with you. You know, to protect you."

Now Ben did laugh.

"Trust me, we were fine," Birdie repeated.

"Where did you go?" Kayla's sudden interest was unnerving.

"What are you doing up, anyway?" Ben asked.

Birdie was glad he avoided her question. This was none of Kayla's business.

Kayla picked up her phone from the nightstand and held it up to them as if they were supposed to see something on the dark screen.

"I couldn't sleep," she said. "My friends back home are having so much fun. And here I am, stuck in this totally dead small town with Grammy and Gramps. I wish someone would just shoot me now."

"*Bruges la morte*," Ben said.

"What?" Kayla said.

"I don't know," Birdie said. "Your grandparents seem okay to me." She rarely saw her own grandparents, especially since the accident.

Kayla gave her a withering look. "You would."

"What's that supposed to mean?"

"Nothing. Now, out with it. Tell me where you were or I'll make up something juicy to tell your uncle and your mom."

"You wouldn't," Ben said, taking a step forward.

"Try me," Kayla said, her blue eyes turning steely.

They stared at each other for a long time.

Finally Birdie broke the standoff.

"If you must know, we went to return that book we found to the boy who dropped it."

"In the middle of the night?"

"Why not?" Ben asked, not dropping his gaze.

"Uh, because you're already in deep with your uncle and she's a miss goody two-shoes who wouldn't sneak out unless she had a life or death reason."

"Guess you were wrong about me," Birdie said smartly.

"Uh, doubtful," Kayla said. "What kind of trouble are you two in, anyway?"

"We're not in any trouble," Ben said. "We just wanted to return the book before Birdie left in the morning."

"Speaking of which," Birdie said, unable to stifle a yawn. "I need to get back upstairs before my mom realizes I'm out of bed."

The light from the hall flooded across the floor of Kayla's room through the slit under the door.

"Too late," Kayla said, jumping up and pulling her door open before Ben or Birdie could protest.

"Hi Mrs. Blessing," Kayla said quietly. "She's in here."

Mrs. Blessing stood in the doorway to Kayla's room in her long lightweight robe.

Birdie's mouth went dry.

"We were playing cards," Kayla said, pointing to a deck of cards on the table next to her bed.

Birdie yawned again. "Probably not the best idea," she

said sheepishly, standing and following her mom out the door and into the hall.

"Probably not," Mrs. Blessing said. "Don't leave the room after lights out again, here or anywhere we stay. Do you understand?"

"Yes. Sorry, Mom."

She didn't turn around but she could sense Ben behind them. A moment later she heard the nearly imperceptible sound of the door closing to his room.

Mrs. Blessing left the conversation there.

Birdie was grateful for that and for the soft bed and the warm covers.

She crawled inside and slept.

"You know those kids snuck out last night, don't you?" Mrs. Blessing said quietly as she pulled a small jar of plain yogurt from the breakfast tray. "Birdie and Ben. I found them in Kayla's room at four in the morning. Kayla said they were playing cards but you don't need sneakers and jackets for that."

"I'm going to kill him," Uncle Noah said. He looked as if he might leave the table immediately to do it.

A smile touched Mrs. Blessing's lips. "Now hold on. They don't know we know. I think it has something to do with that book they found."

"What book?"

"Really?" Mrs. Blessing said. "You didn't notice that giant bulge that's been weighing down the side of Ben's shorts all week?"

"I have no idea what you're talking about."

Mrs. Blessing rolled her eyes. "Let me explain what's been going on."

It was Ben who woke her, rather than her mother. He gripped the book in one hand and his uncle's cellphone in the other.

"How did you get in here?" Birdie asked, sitting up on her elbows.

"Your mom is downstairs having breakfast." He kept his voice low so he wouldn't be overheard by any of the other guests. "She left the door unlocked."

"But why..."

"Birdie, I was doing a little more research online. I think this book may be one of the original copies of *The Game and Playe of the Chesse* that was printed here in Bruges. That's the reason those kids want it - it's valuable and rare. Remember what the girl at the bookstore..."

"Gretchen."

"Yeah, okay, Gretchen. Do you remember what she said?"

"It's the second book ever printed in the English language."

"Exactly. The book was one of a handful printed by William Caxton, the first person to print books in English. He did it here in Bruges. He printed two books in English and then switched to French for a while before moving to England and switching back to English again."

"Eva said the book belonged to Henri's father."

"According to this there are ten remaining copies that have been accounted for," Ben said. "There's a complete copy in the British Library in London, but all the others are incomplete. They're missing pages or damaged."

"So where did this one come from then?"

"I don't know, but listen to this, Birdie. There's an old rumor, never confirmed, that the Beguines once had a complete copy but it was lost."

"The Begijnhof," Birdie said. "It belongs to the sisters. That's why the nun was chasing Henri. So he did steal it from there."

"It would seem so," Ben said. "I can't think of another

explanation."

"So we should return it to the nuns," Birdie grumbled, laying her head back on the soft pillow.

Ben studied her for a moment.

"We should," he said slowly, "you're right. But I haven't told you everything yet. That website, the one that said the Beguines had a copy? Well it also said that there is another rumor that one of the books hid a diary that held a secret to the riches of Venice."

"You're kidding."

"Maybe we should spend some time with it first," Ben said.

"Venice?"

"Yes, Venice. Remember what Mrs. Winggen said? Bruges and Venice were the two big deal ports, the places where riches and treasures came through."

"The handwriting..."

"That's what I was thinking, that the handwriting could be about Venice."

"Did you get a chance to translate any of it?"

Ben shook his head.

"We don't have much time. My mom and I are leaving this afternoon," Birdie said, sitting up and pulling the duvet under her chin. "But don't you think the nuns would've examined this book inside and out if they knew it was supposed to contain that secret? What are we going to find that they didn't?"

"Good point. Still, it doesn't seem right to just hand it over to them. They clearly weren't taking very good care of it. We found it lying on the ground."

"Yeah, except that it belongs to them and not to us or to Henri. What if they think we stole it? We have to return it."

Ben sat down at the foot of her bed and thought for a while.

"I got nothing," he said. He met her eyes and threw his

hands in the air.

"We could go back and ask Henri why he took it," Birdie suggested. "We could retrace our steps from last night."

"Do you really want to go back to that place?" Ben asked.

"No."

"Neither do I."

"But I'm not sure how else to find him again," Birdie said. "His house is, well, unreliable with Mrs. Winggen there, and the dungeon was the last place we saw him."

"But Birdie..."

He stopped when he heard a rustle of wings and air.

"What the?" Ben said, standing.

WOO who.

A dove lighted on the windowsill and bobbed its head at them.

WOO who.

"Birdie," Ben said. "There's a ... bird staring in here."

"Oh, that's just Willy. Don't worry about him. He won't come in," Birdie said.

"Willy?"

"He's been here every morning," Birdie said. "He's a wood pigeon. I thought he was a dove, but he's a plain old pigeon. Apparently pigeons are a type of dove. Or maybe it's vice versa. I don't remember. At least that's what my mom said."

Ben stared at the bird as it bobbed its head. "He has straps on his leg."

"What do you mean?"

"Look, there are little leather straps on his leg, like he had something tied there."

"Like what?"

"I don't know. A note maybe? Or a pouch?"

Willy bobbed his head at them and flew away.

"You should go," Birdie said. "I'll meet you downstairs

in the dining room."

"What?" Ben drew his attention away from Willy. "Oh, yeah. Right. I'll see you down there."

Ben took one last look at Willy, shook his head in disbelief, and then departed.

When she was sure he was gone for good, Birdie slipped out of bed and went into the bathroom to wash up. She pulled on a fresh pair of jeans, then reached down and picked up the pair she'd been wearing the night before. As she cleaned out the pockets, she found the aventurine.

She pulled it out and cupped it in her hand.

The golden knight still shimmered there. She rubbed at it with her thumb but the image remained.

She slipped it into her pocket and then left the room to join her mother downstairs.

The Begijnhof, now the home of
Benedictine nuns, was a safe place
in the Middle Ages for upper-class
unmarried or widowed women who
wanted to dedicate their time to charitable
works. Known as Beguines, they were religious
women who lived together in communities
like the Begijnhof, but were free to leave
the order at any time. Today, their
simple white bungalows and red
brick church still surround
a peaceful courtyard, which
you are free to visit.

Marty McEntire's
Europe for Americans Travel Guide

CHAPTER TWENTY-THREE

When Birdie came downstairs, Ben was already at the table, looking miserable. His uncle and her mom were there, too, along with a family of four she'd never seen before. The mom and dad were sitting where the Hinnershitzes usually sat, which for some reason she found quite irritating.

Birdie slid into her seat beside Ben and picked up an airy croissant from the serving tray in the center of the table.

"Morning," she said.

"Good morning, Birdie," Uncle Noah said. His shaggy hair was combed through this morning, and he was wearing a short-sleeved button-down shirt in place of his usual black t-shirt.

Before Birdie could respond, Mrs. Devon whisked into the dining room through the sliding door.

"Good morning, everyone!" she said, bustling back and forth between them all with a carafe of coffee in one hand and one filled with hot water in the other. "And you must be the Hammersmiths. Welcome to t'Bruges Huis."

The dark-haired father smiled genuinely at Mrs. Devon

and introduced himself as Mark, then introduced his wife, Nancy, who sported a blond bob that was cut razor sharp just below her ears, and their two sons, Nick and Nelson. The boys shared their mother's blond hair and wore crisp-collared polo shirts. They were from Nebraska, Mark explained, and this was their first stop on the continent after a short stay in London. They were following the *Marty McEntire Great Tour of Europe* itinerary.

Uncle Noah and Mrs. Blessing introduced themselves and Ben and Birdie.

"This place is way better than the place we stayed at in London," Nick said, waving his fork to emphasize his point. Birdie put him at about ten. "That was a plain Jane hotel. This place has style." He used the fork to stab a boysenberry pastry from the top tier of the tray.

Nelson, the younger of the two, rolled his eyes.

"Well, I am glad you approve," Mrs. Devon said, and then explained the availability of eggs and bacon. Nick nodded appreciatively and ordered a three-egg omelet. When Mrs. Devon slipped back into the kitchen through the sliding pocket door Nick said to no one in particular, "See? Classy."

Ben tapped Birdie's foot under the table with his skateboarding sneaker. She gulped down a giggle as Ben grinned broadly beside her.

"Don't forget that we're going to the Church of Our Lady this morning," Mrs. Blessing said to Birdie after the Hammersmiths had settled back into their own conversation and Birdie had regained her composure. "Make sure you have all of your stuff packed and stored with Mrs. Devon before we go."

"You're leaving already?" Nick asked. "But we just got here."

"Well, we didn't," Birdie said. "We've been here a few days."

Nick slumped back in his chair.

Ben took his chance. "Mrs. Blessing, Uncle Noah?"

The adults exchanged glances across the table.

"Yes?" Uncle Noah asked, setting down his coffee cup and giving Ben his full attention.

"I know that Mrs. Blessing wants to go to the church this morning, but do you think it would be okay if Birdie and I went on a bike ride after she gets all her stuff packed? She told me about the one she and her mom took and it sounded awesome."

"I don't know that there will be time," Mrs. Blessing said.

"I was thinking maybe we could go while you were studying the Michelangelo statue."

"Ben," Uncle Noah said sternly.

"I just thought since they're leaving..."

"That you'd change their whole itinerary..."

"It's fine by me," Mrs. Blessing said with a sigh.

"Really?" Uncle Noah asked, raising his eyebrows. "After..."

She nodded. "If it's okay with you."

Uncle Noah sat back in his seat, motioning that Mrs. Blessing should take the lead.

She reached into her purse and peeled a few bills from a roll of euros. She handed them to Birdie. "Just do not be late."

"Thanks, Mom," Birdie said.

"Let me get the map," her mother said, pulling it out and opening it up.

"It's okay. We know where the bike rental is and they have maps there if we need them."

Mrs. Blessing refolded the worn map and slipped it into her purse, closing the zippers tightly and latching the small set of hooks that held them closed against the prying fingers of experienced pickpockets.

"Let's plan to meet back here at one o'clock," she said. "Then we can grab our bags, pick up some lunch, and head to the car rental place."

"Uncle Noah?" Ben asked.

He shook his head like he couldn't believe what he was about to say. "Sure, yes. Go ahead. I'll meet you back here at one o'clock."

Birdie and Ben exchanged glances and then stood up. They tossed their napkins onto the table.

"We're going to go then," Birdie said. "Since we don't have much time."

Ben grabbed a large pastry from the top of the tray.

"You heard Mrs. Blessing," Uncle Noah said. "Do not be late."

"Got it. We won't," he said.

Ben and Birdie said their goodbyes to the Hammersmiths and then slipped out through the sitting room.

When they reached the foyer, Kayla swung down the steps and stepped between them.

"And just where are we off to this fine morning?" she asked. She wore a pair of faded jean shorts and a loose-fitting tank top with peach-colored flowers on it. Her feet were barely covered by a pair of strappy leather sandals.

"We?" Ben asked.

"Of course," Kayla replied with a sugary smile. "After that card game last night I thought it would be fun to hang out with you two losers today."

"Come on, then," Birdie said, concerned that if they stayed in the foyer too long her mom, or worse, Uncle Noah, would start asking questions. She pulled the door open and held it for Ben and Kayla.

"So, where are we going?" Kayla asked after the door closed behind them.

"We're retracing our steps from last night," Ben said, starting off at a fast clip and turning when they reached the alley.

"Do you really think that's a good idea?" Kayla asked.

Neither Birdie nor Ben answered her.

"Do you remember the way?" Ben asked when they reached the intersection where Henri and Mary had run from the boys. Birdie nodded and led the way past the buildings that had loomed so dark the night before.

They reached the wall that bordered the main canal, passing from sun to shadow as they moved under trees with large canopies of leaves. Kayla struggled to keep up with them. A few minutes later they arrived at the stone bridge.

"There," Birdie pointed across the canal to the park and the buildings beyond. "That's where we went."

"Where?" Kayla asked. "To the Minnewater?"

The park that stretched before them was as serene a place as could be, made even more peaceful by the rays of morning sun that whisked away the mist. Except for swans and ducks, it was deserted this early in the morning.

"Follow me," Ben said. He led them across the park, past the tree where they'd found the book, and through the iron gate.

"This is the Begijnhof," Kayla said. "See those little white bungalows? That's where the Beguines lived, or at least they used to. Now the Benedictine nuns live there. And that's their church. My grandparents dragged me out of bed and over here the other morning."

They crossed the courtyard with the overgrown grass and tall trees.

When they reached the gate on the far end, it was closed and locked.

Kayla pulled out her phone. "Nine-fifteen," she said. "They don't open that gate for the tourists to come in until nine-thirty."

"Then why was the other gate open?" Birdie asked, pointing to the one they had just crossed through. "And they were both wide open last night."

"I don't know," Kayla said. "It probably has something to do with the church."

The bell in the steeple tolled once.

"It's a service," Kayla said. She started walking toward the tall arched doorway that led into the church.

"What are you doing?" Ben asked.

"I was going to go in," Kayla said, stopping and looking at Ben and Birdie. "There's no way to get through that gate for another fifteen minutes and unless you know another way past it I thought I'd rather sit on a chair in the cool air of the church than bake out here in the sun."

Birdie checked her watch.

"Okay," she said. "But not a minute longer."

They followed a roughly cobbled path to the entrance. Kayla pulled the heavy wooden door open and they stepped inside.

The tall sanctuary was dim and smoky, as if candles had just been blown out. Straight wooden chairs, rather than pews, were lined up in three sections. The main sanctuary faced the biggest altar, and two smaller chapels faced smaller altars that flanked each side. The service was underway and the priest's recitation reached them without the help of amplification.

Kayla moved across the dark tiled floor all the way to the small chapel on the right and sat down in an empty seat in the front row. Birdie and Ben sat beside her. To their left a tray of candles in different sizes and various stages of melting threw light into the dim space.

"They're prayers," Kayla whispered. "You buy a candle and light it for your prayer. Usually they're in honor or memory of people."

"How do you know?" Birdie asked.

"Grammy and Gramps love going to churches. Grammy lights a candle in memory of each of the dogs they've had."

"Really?" Birdie whispered. Kayla nodded.

"Consolation," Ben said quietly.

"What?" Birdie asked.

"That's what this little side chapel is. The Chapel of Consolation." He was reading a leaflet that had been left on the chair.

Birdie picked hers up and found the section with the English translation.

"To bring peace to those who are lost and console those who mourn," it read.

In front of them a statue of the Virgin Mary holding Baby Jesus sat among flowers and greens.

Birdie closed her eyes and bowed her head.

She breathed in the still air, heavy with the fragrance of candle wax and incense. In the main sanctuary the organ began to play and the sisters began to sing.

She couldn't understand the words they said, but she recognized the ritual, the repetition, the cadence of the hymns.

She allowed thoughts of Jonah and her father to come, to sit with her on her slender wooden chair at the altar of consolation.

This time she didn't push them away.

The last time she'd been at a church service it had been their funeral. She'd walked behind their caskets as they were taken to be buried together on the hill in the town cemetery.

Now they would be there together, forever.

"We all have to die sometime, Birdie."

Birdie's eyes flew open. She looked at Kayla, then at Ben. They were both staring off into the church, lost in their own thoughts.

She looked up at the statue of the Virgin Mary.

It was just marble and wood.

Had she really heard something? Or was it her imagination, a trick of the light and the candles and the centuries-old chapel?

The music swelled around her as the service came to an end.

The bells in the steeple high above them began to chime. "Nine-thirty," Ben whispered.

Kayla nodded. "The gate should be opening. Let's go."

"Wait," Birdie said. "Hold on a second."

She dug in her pocket for the money her mother had given her for the bike, then stood up and approached the tray of burning candles. A spiral stand next to the tray held the largest candles of all. They were in glass jars nearly eight inches tall and looked as if they would burn for days. Each one cost five euros.

Birdie folded the bill and pushed it into the slit on the top of the metal offering box, then selected a tall white candle. She used a piece of wick to light it, then placed it on the very top rung of the spiral holder.

She watched it burn for a moment.

"Time to go," Kayla said behind her.

Birdie nodded.

When she turned away from the candle, Ben was watching her.

"For my dad and my brother," she said.

Ben nodded and followed her from the church.

CHAPTER TWENTY-FOUR

The sky outside the church was bright. Birdie had to shield her eyes against the sunshine after the deep shadows of the chapel.

On the far end of the clearing, the iron gate now stood open.

"Let's do this," Ben said.

As it had last night, the gate led to a clearing surrounded by a hedge. The fountain gurgled in the center. In their rush the night before Birdie hadn't noticed the larger, paved path that led to the gate from the other direction. This morning dozens of tourists were congregating on it and filing through the gate to see the place where the Beguines once lived.

They crossed the clearing and ducked under the hedge on the far side.

"This bush looks different than it did last night," Birdie said, standing up and brushing needles from her jacket. "It's bigger. And pricklier."

Ben pointed to the narrow footpath that bordered the canal. "Come on. This way."

They walked a few yards down the path until they

reached the archway that Henri had pulled Mary through the night before. Ben checked to make sure no one was watching them, then passed under the stone arch into the darkened stairwell. Birdie followed, with Kayla at her heels.

"Hold," Ben said, stopping abruptly.

Birdie didn't realize how close they were on the spiral staircase and slammed into his back. A moment later, Kayla plowed into her.

"Ow!" Birdie cried, unable to stop the sound before it left her lips.

"Shh," Ben whispered. Birdie felt him turn toward her in the dark but she couldn't see a thing.

"What is it?" she whispered back.

"I don't know. I thought I heard something." Ben cracked open the door and stepped into the dungeon with Birdie close behind.

"Oh, for goodness sakes," Kayla said, pushing past them in the dark.

A moment later the chamber was flooded with a bright white light.

Birdie blinked, ready to turn and run.

"Now we can see where we're going," Kayla said, holding up her phone so the bright stream of her flashlight app swept over the long corridor.

"It's a bar," Kayla said.

Birdie blinked again.

"Yes!" Ben said as he stepped past them. "It's the Monk Bar. Birdie, didn't I tell you that last night? I could have sworn it was the place where Uncle Noah and I had dinner. They call it the Monk Bar because they only carry beer brewed by monks. I thought it was the same place because of the arches. I know there are a ton of places with old arches in this town, but I spent so much time staring at these while Uncle Noah quizzed the bartender that I recognized the pattern of the stones."

There was no sign of the children they'd seen the night before.

There was no fire in the center to warm the cold stone slabs.

The arched alcoves cocooned tables and chairs instead of bedding and clothes, candles and children. A polished wooden bar with a dozen high-backed stools lined the far wall, with just enough space for a bartender to maneuver behind it.

"What is going on?" Birdie said. She took a few steps into the corridor and peered behind one of the arches, half expecting to see a pile of rags and children, but there were only more tables and chairs.

They were the only ones in the barroom, fortunately, since it was still too early for the bar backs to arrive to slice lemons and limes and prepare for the afternoon rush. The smoky, sausage-scented air from the night before was replaced with a dank combination of yesterday's beer and something less pleasant, like the steam from the sewer grates they passed from time to time up above.

"This isn't what it looked like last night," Birdie explained to Kayla.

"Are you sure you weren't sleepwalking?" Kayla swept the light around the empty bar.

"Both of us?" Birdie said. "Not likely."

"Maybe you were dreaming."

"Because Birdie and I are telepathically connected and would have the exact same dream about a place that apparently doesn't even exist," Ben said.

"Well," Kayla said, raising her eyebrows at both of them, "then how do you explain the fact that this place miraculously changed? Are you sure you had the right hedge?"

"Kayla, do you want to hang out with us or not?" Ben asked. "If you do, then you might want to shut the hell up.

We're trying to figure this out."

Kayla looked like she was going to say something snarky, but then her shoulders sagged and she shook her head slightly.

"Fine," she said. "So then let me help. If this place didn't look like this last night, what did it look like?"

"It wasn't a bar, for starters," Birdie said. "It was an, an, orphanage almost. But no adults. There were children here. Lots of children. And a girl named Eva. I talked with her. She's the one who said I had to return the book or else."

"Or else what?"

"I don't know," Birdie said, but a shiver ran up her arms at the memory of Eva touching her. "It was really creepy, okay? I just wanted to get out of there and I didn't prolong it by asking a lot of questions."

She shoved her hands in the pocket of her jacket. The aventurine was there, warm against her skin. She tumbled it in her pocket nervously, and then brought it out to look at it. The knight was still there.

"What is that?" Kayla asked, snatching it from Birdie's hand.

"Hey!" Birdie said. "Give that back."

Kayla turned the aventurine over in her palm.

"It's hot," she said, dropping it back into Birdie's outstretched hand.

"It was in my pocket," Birdie said.

"Okay," Kayla said, the aventurine forgotten. "So this isn't the same place you losers were last night. This is the bar and unless we do want trouble, we'd better get out of here. I don't want to get arrested in Belgium for trespassing."

Ben ignored her. He walked forward, deeper into the chamber.

"Here, let me see that," he said, holding out his hand for Kayla's phone.

She hesitated and then handed it to him. "Don't drop it."

Ben used the light on the phone to inspect each alcove. When he reached the end of the corridor he turned around, temporarily blinding them before pointing the light back down to the floor.

"There's nothing here except tables and chairs," he said. "I just don't understand it. Sorry Birdie."

A key scraped in the lock of a large door behind the bar not far from where Ben was standing. His eyes grew wide as he sprinted back across the room. As he grabbed Birdie by the arm and began to pull her toward the door, the light on the phone went black.

"What the ... did you drop..." Kayla's words fell away as she turned to face them. She stared past them.

Birdie's eyes slowly adjusted to the dim light. She and Ben turned to follow Kayla's gaze.

"You came back," Eva said, walking toward them.

She was dressed as she had been the night before but with her hair swept across her shoulder in a long plait. She held out her hand.

No one moved.

"Who are you?" she asked, sizing up Kayla. "And where are your clothes?"

"I could ask you the same thing," Kayla said. Birdie thought her voice sounded shakier than normal.

"I am Eva." She turned to Ben and Birdie. "The book?"

"We are looking for Henri," Birdie said, taking a step forward.

"He is not here."

"Then we'll be back with the book after we find him."

Eva laughed, throwing her head back for a moment, and then meeting Birdie straight in the eye. "I will take the book now."

"I don't have it," she said.

"I am aware of that," Eva said, taking a step closer to Birdie. When she did, Kayla moved between them.

"Now hold up there, Eva, that book doesn't belong to you," she said.

Eva ignored Kayla and raised her voice to call out something in what sounded like Dutch. A moment later the group of boys who'd been playing dice the night before stepped out of the alcoves and flanked her on either side.

Jan grinned at Birdie.

Every instinct told her to take a step back, but she held firm.

"I will ask again," Eva said smoothly. "The book."

No one said anything.

Then Kayla took another step forward, her chin held high.

"That would be a no," Kayla said, her hands going to her hips. "There is no way in hell we're giving you anything." She looked beyond Eva and the boys. "What is this place anyway?"

Eva murmured something in another language. It wasn't the French or Dutch that Birdie was coming to recognize even if she didn't understand it. This sounded older and very different.

As Eva's voice died away she stepped forward and grabbed Kayla by the arm.

"Hey," Kayla cried, as she tried to shake off the thinner girl's grasp. "Let me go!"

The boys circled behind them and Jan grabbed Ben by his arms, yanking him back away from Birdie. Ben fought against them, but Jan and his gang began dragging him down the long corridor, past the alcoves flickering with candlelight.

Ben thrashed against their grasp but he was outnumbered. He couldn't break free.

Jan grabbed the pocket of Ben's cargo shorts and tore it

straight down.

The book tumbled onto the floor.

The boy who looked like a rat swept in and picked up the book with a dirty hand.

"Eva," he called.

Eva stopped her argument with Kayla long enough to look his way. When she did, he tossed the book across the chamber to her.

Eva gave him a wide grin as she caught it easily. She said something to him that sounded appreciative. She called him Joos.

Joos nodded as he caught up with the other boys, looking pleased with himself.

Eva turned her attention back to Kayla as the boys continued to drag Ben through the corridor.

"Hey! Where do you think you're taking him?" Birdie yelled at them. "You got your stupid book back, now let him go!"

The boys acted as if she hadn't said a word.

She took off after them, the footfalls of her sneakered feet nearly silent on the cobblestone floor.

Kayla and Eva were shouting at each other behind her, their voices echoing through the cold stone arches.

Birdie caught up to the boys quickly. She reached out with both hands and grabbed Joos by the scruff of his coat collar.

She yanked him back as hard as she could.

She'd caught him off-guard. He fell back toward her and lost his grip on Ben.

Birdie pivoted to the left to avoid his fall and went after Jan as Ben regained his footing and began to break free. She grabbed Jan by his collar and pulled as she'd done to Joos, but he proved heavier and was distracted by trying to hold onto Ben, who was now seconds away from breaking free.

Jan yelled something that Birdie didn't understand.

Several alcoves ahead of them the boys who were leading the way turned around.

When they saw what was happening they reversed course and charged at Ben. The tallest one punched Ben hard in the jaw while a short stubby one grabbed his free arm and began dragging him even harder. Ben kicked with his skateboarding sneakers but couldn't gain any traction on the cobbled floor.

Birdie didn't let go of Jan and he thrashed in her grasp. She struggled to hold him.

"Let Ben go!" she cried. As she did, a set of heavy hands circled her waist and pulled her backward, hard. Jan's collar slipped from her hands. A moment later she found herself face down on the floor, gasping for the air that had been knocked out of her.

She rolled over and saw Joos laughing as he ran to catch up with the boys who were holding Ben. They all seemed to shimmer as he approached.

"Ben!" she cried, but her voice sounded funny, even to herself.

It was too late.

She tried to scramble to her feet but her head throbbed and the best she could do was sit up.

She searched the dimly lit corridor, but it was no use.

Ben was gone.

CHAPTER TWENTY-FIVE

"No," Birdie said, closing her eyes and rubbing the knot that was forming on her forehead where she'd knocked it against an uneven stone.

An alarm was sounding somewhere nearby, piercing the air and then silencing as quickly as it had started.

"Birdie, let's go."

It was Kayla. She tugged on Birdie's arm. "We need to go. Now."

Birdie opened her eyes.

She gasped.

They were back in the bar. The cobblestone floor now supported a maze of chair and table legs. Kayla's phone was once again throwing a bright circle of light around them.

"Come on, Birdie. Someone's coming." Kayla nearly dropped her phone trying to kill the light.

As Birdie struggled to her feet, she heard a door sliding open. It sounded like it was coming from the other side of the room behind the bar.

Kayla slipped an arm under her shoulder and they started back toward the door where they'd entered.

"But Ben..." Birdie began, looking over her shoulder.

"He's not here," Kayla said, pulling her along.

The room flooded with light.

Birdie and Kayla froze just steps from the door that led to the spiral staircase and freedom.

A bar back came in through a door behind the bar and clicked on more overhead lights. He was jamming to music on his headphones and hadn't noticed them. When he turned his back to grab something from behind the bar, they slipped through the door.

"Are you okay?" Kayla asked when they'd climbed the stairs and cleared the other side of the hedge.

Birdie collapsed on the damp grass.

"Oh my God. Oh ... my ... God. Kayla. Ben is gone. They have Ben. What are we going to do? What are they going to do? Oh my God!"

"Birdie," Kayla said sternly. "Snap out of it. We're going to figure this out." She looked around the clearing and then back at the hedge. "Whatever the hell this is."

"We need to find him," Birdie said.

"What about the book?"

"Who cares about the stupid book? We can't go back without Ben. We need to get back in there."

Birdie tried to stand up again but Kayla put a hand on her shoulder and sat down beside her.

"What we need is a plan," Kayla said. "We need to think. Think first, then act."

"I think we need to go back in there and get Ben!"

"I think we should try to find the kid you were talking about."

"They could be hurting him. They probably are hurting him. What am I going to tell his uncle?"

"Birdie. Concentrate. We need to find the kid who hid the book in the first place. He's our best bet for getting Ben back. He'll know those kids and he'll know his way around that dungeon. Now think." She shook her hard by the shoulders. "Where would he be?"

"Henri?" Birdie swiped at her eyes where tears were forming.

"Yes, right. Henri. What's been the common link when you saw Henri?"

Birdie tried to think but her mind just raced.

What were they going to do to Ben?

"Birdie?"

"I don't know," she said, shaking her head.

Kayla gave her a stern look.

A fat tear escaped from Birdie's right eye and slid down her cheek.

"We are never going to find Ben if you can't pull yourself together. Now quit crying and think."

"Okay, fine," Birdie said, rubbing her face with her hands and then looking up at Kayla. "He waves."

"Okay, that's good," Kayla said encouragingly. "He waves. He waves when you see him?"

"Yes. He always waves to us."

"Is there anything happening before you see him? Something that happens every time? Are you always in the same place?"

Birdie stared at the water cascading through the fountain and tried to concentrate on the question.

"The first time I saw him," she said, "Ben and I were on the roof of the brewery. He was in the park and an old woman - a nun we think - was chasing him."

"Okay, good. What about the next time?"

Birdie explained her encounters with Henri on the canal cruise, in the alley by t'Bruges Huis, and on the street in front of his house.

"Wait, you know where he lives?" Kayla asked unable to keep the excitement from her voice as she rocked up onto her knees. "Let's go get him."

"No, Kayla, he doesn't actually live there," Birdie said, shaking her head. "Well, I'm not sure if he lives there."

"Damn it, Birdie, do you know where he lives or not?"

"I saw him go into this house. His little sister was there, too. Her name is Mary. But then when Ben and I went there to find him the only person home was Mrs. Winggen and she swears there are no children in the house and there haven't been for years."

"Okay," Kayla said in a tone that made it clear that she didn't really think Birdie was okay. "Let's see. What else might matter?"

She thought for a while. Then her eyes lit up.

"Did you always have the book with you when you saw him?"

"No."

"Did he always have the book?"

"No."

The light in her eyes dimmed. Kayla thought some more.

"Was Ben always with you?"

"Yes," Birdie said. "No, wait. He wasn't with me on the canal cruise. My mom was."

"What does Henri look like?" Kayla asked.

"He looks ... different," Birdie said. "He wears these thick pants that are kind of like tights really and that are too wide and too long at the same time. His feet are almost always bare and when they're not he wears shoes that are too big for him and look kind of like moccasins. His shirt is white and I think it has some kind of hooks instead of buttons. His hair is shaggy and sandy blond, and his eyes are green. He's a little shorter than me, but I think he's older than me or at least my same age."

Kayla considered Birdie's answer as they sat together on the grass. A few more people had entered the clearing, but none of them seemed particularly interested in Birdie and Kayla.

Birdie looked back toward the hedge, hoping against hope that she'd see Ben crawling through it.

There was no one there.

"I don't know what to say, Birdie. From what you described, it's almost like he's from another time. And that creepy dungeon we were in ... I don't even know what to think about that place. And how did it change..."

"What did you say?" Birdie asked, sitting up straighter.

"The creepy dungeon..."

"No, before that."

"I said I thought it sounded like Henri was from a different time."

Birdie stood up.

"What?" Kayla asked.

"That's it."

"What is it?"

"Of course." Birdie reached into her jacket pocket. "That's how we can find Henri. That's how we can get back to Ben."

"What are you talking about?"

"The aventurine. The piece of Venetian glass."

Birdie pulled the cinnamon-colored oval from her pocket and held it in the palm of her hand.

"That little stone?" Kayla asked. "How?"

"I'm not sure," Birdie admitted. "I don't understand how it works." She thought about the legend they'd read in the brewery gift shop. "I'm not sure I'm supposed to understand. But it led Ben and me to the book, so maybe it will lead us to Henri."

As she spoke, the knight dissolved and the gold sparkles began swirling again.

She rubbed the aventurine and they swirled faster. When the glass grew too hot to hold she dropped it on the grass between them.

"What's it doing?" Kayla asked, her eyes growing wide.

"Just watch."

The gold shimmered and swirled. It seemed to take forever to finally decide on a shape, but when it did all the gold flew into the coppery center.

"What is it?" Kayla asked.

"It's a coat of arms," Birdie said. "And I've seen it before. Somewhere here in Bruges."

"I know where," Kayla said, standing up and brushing the dirt from her bare legs. "It hangs outside t'Bruges Huis. On the sign that swings out front."

"You're right! Come on!"

Birdie and Kayla sprinted along the narrow cobblestone streets, skirting tourist groups on the way. When they reached the lane they slowed.

Kayla stopped a few houses away from t'Bruges Huis.

"Hold on," she panted, bending to put her hands on her knees.

Birdie ignored her and approached the wood and metal sign that swayed out front.

There it was, the coat of arms with a standing bear holding a B.

Maybe Ben was inside. Maybe he'd made it back somehow.

Or Henri. Maybe Henri was here, inside with Mary waiting for them in the sitting room.

She pulled the aventurine from her pocket and held it up.

No.

It couldn't be.

"See," Kayla said, reaching her side still out of breath. "There it is."

"No," Birdie said, thrusting the aventurine under Kayla's

nose. "It's not the same. The bear is different. The one on the glass is wearing armor and its shield doesn't have a B on it."

"It's so close, though," Kayla said, studying the two images.

Birdie rubbed the aventurine but the standing bear held fast.

"Let's go inside anyway." Kayla leaned against the wall of the house next door. "Maybe it's close enough. The symbol could have changed with time."

They took a few steps toward the front door.

Birdie stopped and held her finger to her lips to silence Kayla. She pointed to the front windows of t'Bruges Huis. They were tilted open just a bit to let the cool breeze pass through the house. Voices floated out to them from inside.

"So you're telling me that Benny and Birdie came to your house?" It was Uncle Noah. As usual he did not sound happy. "When was this?"

"Yesterday, in the afternoon." There was no mistaking Mrs. Winggen's tinker bell voice. "We had a lovely tea together. They're really quite well behaved children. You should be proud of yourselves. Oh thank you, dear."

"You're welcome, Mrs. Winggen." It was Mrs. Devon. Birdie wondered what she was doing there so late in the morning.

"Yes, thank you," Mrs. Blessing repeated.

"Let me know if you need anything else," Mrs. Devon said.

Birdie recognized the sound of a teacup gently joining its saucer. She didn't dare to stand up on her tiptoes to look in the window. She and Kayla crouched low beneath the ledge.

"Why weren't they with you?" Uncle Noah asked after the pocket door clicked closed. Birdie couldn't see into the sitting room, but she assumed he was talking to her mom.

Mrs. Blessing didn't answer him and instead asked, "Why did they come to see you?"

"It was the strangest thing," Mrs. Winggen said. "They were looking for another boy. I told them no boys had lived in the house for ages, of course."

Mrs. Winggen continued for several minutes, explaining the home's lineage and talking about her daughters.

Kayla threw a questioning look at Birdie, who shrugged and held her finger up. "Just wait," she mouthed.

Mrs. Blessing gently steered the older woman back to the matter at hand. "Was that all Ben and Birdie wanted, Mrs. Winggen? To see if the boy lived at your house?"

No one spoke for a long time. Birdie could hear the porcelain cups and saucers clinking. Then Mrs. Winggen continued.

"They had a book with them. An old, leather-bound book."

"Yes, I've seen them looking at something like that," Mrs. Blessing said.

"You see, after they left I climbed up to the attic and pulled out an old family ledger. I'd nearly forgotten that I had it up there. I don't climb those stairs very often now with the arthritis in my knees. The doctor says..."

Mrs. Blessing cleared her throat.

"Oh, yes, right. Well, the ledger was up there. It's one of those things that belongs to the house if you can understand that. It will stay with it as long as the house stands. It's quite heavy and..."

"What did you find in the ledger?" Uncle Noah asked.

"Oh, yes, it was quite interesting. It turns out there was a gentleman named Henri LeFort who lived in the house. He claimed it back in 1515. Not many people had much use for Bruges by then. The town's time had passed." There was a pause, then Birdie heard the cup clink with the saucer again.

"Let's see. He would have been my great-grandfather

many times over. The *Witte Beertje Huis* - our houses had names then, you see, it was long before they thought to give them numbers. In English it means White Bear House. Yes, so Witte Beertje Huis had been vacant for more than a decade by the time Henri came to Bruges with his sister, Mary. I imagine it was in a sorry state. Why he would want it I don't know, but he claimed he had a right to it.

"There are notes in the ledger, the handwriting is very small and neat, that say the Aldermen didn't believe him at first. He and Mary had been listed in the town archives as being sent to France to live with an uncle after their parents died, with a note that they'd never arrived. They were presumed to be dead, of course, two children out on their own. How horrible it must have been for them. You would think some of the Aldermen would have noticed Henri's resemblance to his father since his father had been an Alderman himself. But they didn't, I suppose. So much had changed by then. So many people had died and so many had abandoned the town. There was so much violence here after the ships stopped coming to Bruges."

Birdie heard the cup clink against the saucer again.

"In the end there was no proof that it wasn't his family's house," Mrs. Winggen continued, "and because it had been vacant for so long the Aldermen waved their argument. An occupied house meant taxes in the coffers, you see. My family has lived in Witte Beertje Huis ever since."

Mrs. Winggen began to talk about her mother and father.

Birdie motioned to Kayla and they moved quietly down the lane. When they were a few houses away Birdie stopped.

"I wonder," she whispered.

You'll see coats of arms
all over Bruges -on public buildings,
on private houses, even in the churches.
The families of the merchants were very
important to the town, and each family
had its own coat of arms. They were
positioned in different places around
Bruges in their honor, and to remind
people who was in charge.

Marty McEntire's
Europe for Americans Travel Guide

CHAPTER TWENTY-SIX

"What?" Kayla asked.

"Let's go to Henri's house."

"I thought you said he doesn't really live there?"

"Just ... come on."

"Remind me to wear different shoes the next time I decide to go out with you," Kayla grumbled as she adjusted the straps on her kitten-heeled sandals. Birdie could see angry red blisters forming beneath the thin leather.

They backtracked along the canal and across the bridge until they reached the lane where Henri's house sat. Birdie stopped and pulled the aventurine from her pocket. She rubbed it hard and it grew hot.

"Look, Kayla," she said, pointing to the house where Henri lived.

The flowers were red and purple again.

"There's the bear!" Kayla said. A coat of arms with the bear standing proud in its armor peeked out from beneath the flowers on the front of each window box.

Birdie held up the aventurine. The images matched perfectly.

"You're right!"

Birdie sprinted up to the front door with Kayla close behind her. She pulled the long iron bell. Its chime echoed inside.

Quick steps sounded behind the door. A peephole slid open, and then, a moment later, the latch clicked and the heavy door was pulled inward. Birdie stepped inside the vestibule, with Kayla on her heels.

"Henri," Birdie said as the door closed behind them. The boy nodded at Birdie and eyed Kayla cautiously.

They followed him through the interior door and into the foyer. Light shone through the stained glass windows and created a lovely pattern on the wooden floor just as it had the day before when she and Ben had tea with Mrs. Winggen.

But today the house was different. The air inside was heavy with dust, creosote, and age. Rays of sun flooded through the parlor, picking up the layers of dust that hung thick in the air. Hulking furniture hid beneath heavy sheets.

Henri stood beside them in the foyer, while Mary sat on the parlor's bare floor near an anemic flame that flickered behind the fireplace grate. Despite the spring-like weather outside, it felt cold and damp within the thick walls of the medieval home.

"*Mon livre?*" he asked.

"I ... we don't have it anymore," Birdie said, understanding the French words for *my book* after hearing them so many times. "We need your help to get it back."

"Back?"

Birdie nodded. "From Eva. Eva took it from Ben. Her gang of boys did it. And they took Ben, too."

Henri's green eyes grew wide and fear flickered across them.

Birdie's stomach sank.

"Are they the same boys who chased you the other

night?" Birdie asked.

"Non," Henri said, shaking his head. "They are worse. That is why I went into the..." he paused, searching for the English word, "*cave. La cave pour du vin.* Wine."

Confusion must have crossed Birdie's face because Henri continued without mentioning wine again.

"They are loyal to Eva."

"Are you loyal to Eva?" Birdie asked.

"*Non!*" Henri said, growing agitated. "Never to Eva."

"But she protected you. From those boys."

"I pay for Eva's protection. That is why she wants the book."

"As payment?"

"*Oui.*"

"For what?"

Henri didn't answer. Instead he asked, "Where is the book now?"

As Birdie explained what happened, speaking painfully slowly to make sure Henri understood the situation, Kayla moved into the parlor and lowered herself to the dusty floor beside Mary.

"Hello," Kayla said, her voice soft and light.

Mary's eyes darted to Henri.

He nodded.

"*Hallo,*" she whispered.

Kayla traced her finger on the dusty floor. "My name is Kayla."

"Mary."

"That's a pretty name."

Birdie had no idea whether Mary understood the compliment, but she rewarded Kayla with a wisp of a smile. Her petite face looked more childlike at that moment than it had at any other time Birdie had seen her.

Kayla drew a circle on the floor with her finger and added big round eyes. She looked at Mary expectantly.

Mary placed a tiny finger in the dust and drew the curve of a smiling mouth.

Kayla added a nose.

Mary studied the face and began to add sweeps of long hair. It would be a girl.

"So Ben is gone? You do not know where?" Henri asked.

"He was at the dungeon ... the cave. That's the last place we saw him."

"We must go back," Henri said. "Those boys are dangerous."

"But what will we do?"

Henri walked into the parlor and tugged on a heavy sheet. It slipped just a little, revealing a beautiful bureau. He pulled open the top drawer and retrieved something small, which he quickly slipped into his pocket before covering the elegant piece of furniture again.

"We must go," he said.

Mary stood immediately, the hem of her heavy skirt falling to her ankles. She offered a tiny hand to Kayla.

Kayla laced her fingers with Mary's and stood. They followed Henri and Birdie back out onto the street.

Kayla gasped.

The cobblestone lane was nearly empty, except for a pair of horses drawing an over-full wagon at the far end. The canal held a string of skinny barges loaded down with goods. The scent of the sea and humanity and smoke laced into an unlikely perfume.

Henri bowed his head and hugged the facades of the buildings as they passed, trying to make himself as inconspicuous as possible. Birdie followed him closely as they entered the park and then passed through the iron gate into the Begijnhof courtyard.

"*Vous! Garçon!*"

The aged voice cracked as if coming to them through ancient stereo speakers. Birdie turned to see that the source of the words was a petite nun in heavy black robes.

Henri shouted, *"Cours! Run!"*

They took off after Henri at a fast clip, crossing beneath the tall trees in the courtyard and passing through the gate on the other end. They sprinted across the clearing, through the opening in the hedge, and down the narrow dirt path before ducking under the archway.

"That was the nun you stole the book from," Birdie whispered when they reached the door at the bottom of the stairs. Kayla pulled up behind her, panting. Mary stayed tucked up beside the older girl.

"Stole?" Henri's quiet voice sounded incredulous. "It is my book. *Mon pere...* My father bought that book. It is that Beguine who stole it from me!"

"The Beguine? You mean the nun? But why?" Birdie asked.

"For the gold, of course," Henri whispered. "The printer has moved to England and his books are rare. My parents ... they are gone. The Beguines at the Begijnhof were ordered by the Aldermen to care for us until they found *Maman's* family in France. *Non.* The Beguines will steal all we have left."

"How do you know?" Birdie asked.

Henri didn't answer.

"Will you go to France?" she asked.

"*Non. Maman's* family is *la morte,* dead. The plague took them, too."

"What will you do?"

"Mary and I will leave Bruges with all that we can carry as soon as we can make safe passage."

"To where?"

"Shhh." Henri held up his hand. He pressed his ear to the door.

"He is still alive," he whispered.

"You can hear him?"

"*Oui.*"

Birdie's pulse quickened. "Does he sound okay?"

"He is playing cards."

"Cards?" Kayla asked. "Seriously?"

"Follow me." Henri pushed the door open.

They entered the dimly lit chamber in silence and took a step forward.

It took a moment for their eyes to adjust.

Under the stone arches at the end of the long corridor, the boys Birdie fought with earlier in the day were sitting on the floor. Henri was right. They were playing cards. Ben was with them, his right eye bruised and swollen. His bottom lip was fat and decorated by a trail of dried blood leading down his chin.

"Now you," he was saying, "want to lay down this one."

He repeated the sentence in French and Jan dropped a card on the pile with sausage-like fingers.

Birdie felt movement behind her and watched, unable to say a word without drawing attention to herself, as Mary led Kayla away down a narrow side hall toward the alcoves. She caught Kayla's eyes as they passed.

"It's okay," Kayla whispered.

Henri and Birdie watched in silence as the card game unfolded. Ben instructed Jan and a younger boy he called Jacob on their moves.

The lump on Birdie's head throbbed at the sight of them.

"*Regarde!*" Henri cried.

Before Birdie could look where Henri was pointing, a snarling voice rose up from behind them.

"Well look who's back."

Birdie spun and found herself face to face with the rat-faced teenager, Joos, his long hair reaching his shoulders and his teeth dark and crooked behind thin, scarred lips. She could hear the boys behind her getting to their feet.

Henri addressed Joos in Dutch. Birdie had no idea what

he was saying, but even from across the room she could tell that Ben was listening intently. She wondered if he understood Dutch as well as he did French.

After a moment's conversation, Henri pulled out the item he'd retrieved from the bureau drawer. To Birdie's amazement it was a sparkling green jewel the size of a pencil eraser.

Joos eyed the jewel and then snatched it from Henri's palm. He placed it between his teeth and bit down. When nothing happened he pulled it from his mouth and nodded at Henri, murmuring something that sounded appreciative. Then he turned away from them and began to walk toward the card game. When Birdie and Henri fell into step behind him, he wheeled around and struck.

Birdie dodged his fist and landed the hardest kick she could on his kneecap. Her sneakers softened the blow, but it was enough to knock him off balance. As he stumbled, Henri pushed him hard.

Joos yelled and the other boys abandoned the card game.

Everything happened quickly then.

The jewel tumbled from Joos's hand and Henri scooped it up. Behind them, a girl's scream filled the corridor, followed by a heavy thud. Birdie didn't dare to take her eyes off the pack of boys who were bearing down on them. Ben, forgotten in the commotion, struggled to his feet. His arms were tied uncomfortably behind his back but he started toward them anyway.

There was movement all around them then as Birdie and Henri each ducked down and reached a leg out to trip Jan and Jacob. A moment later Ben was by their side.

As the boys scrambled to their feet, Ben, Birdie and Henri sprinted to the door.

CHAPTER TWENTY-SEVEN

Henri threw the door open and they flew up the spiral
staircase. A moment later they passed through the archway
and were blinded by the sunlight. They ducked under the
hedge and kept going, worried that the boys were on their
heels.

They sprinted across the courtyard and through the iron
gate, weaving through the stands of windswept trees. They'd
almost cleared them when someone reached out from
behind a tree and snagged Henri by the collar, yanking him
backward and nearly off his feet.

"*Le livre*," they heard a woman say.

Ben and Birdie slowed, stopped, and spun around.

The Beguine was small, no more than five feet tall,
dressed in long black robes with thick white scarves covering
the sides of her face and neck. Her head was concealed by a
large black hood that stood out firmly on each side, as if
there were a small umbrella inside holding it up.

The boys emerged from behind the hedge with Eva at
their side, her cheek split open and blood dripping down her
face. When they saw the Beguine holding Henri they

stopped dead. Eva murmured something and they retreated back toward the dungeon in slow motion, as if terrified of being seen.

Birdie hurried to untie Ben's wrists.

Meanwhile the Beguine was turning out Henri's pockets.

"*Non, Madame, s'il vous plaît!*" Henri protested, twisting in her grasp.

Birdie saw a flash of green as the jewel in Henri's pocket broke loose from the fabric and tumbled to the ground. Henri shifted his foot to cover it.

The Beguine said something in Dutch and then let him go with a rough push. Henri held his footing. She said something else to him, and he bowed his head deeply.

The Beguine turned away, but did not rush to leave. She glided away from Henri, who stood rooted to the spot. He stayed there until she reached the small gate that led to her whitewashed bungalow and disappeared behind it.

"What was that all about?" Ben asked after Henri scooped up the jewel and ran to catch up to him and Birdie.

"*Où est Mary?*" He looked around the courtyard. "Where is my sister?"

"She was with Kayla," Birdie said, instinctively taking a step back toward the dungeon. "We need to..."

"No, Birdie." Ben stuck his arm out in front of her to block the way. "If you're fixing to go back in that place you can forget it right now."

The concern on his battered face stopped her in her tracks.

"Mary knows where to hide," Henri said, hesitating a moment before starting to walk again. "She knows where to meet me."

"So you're just going to leave her here?" Birdie placed her hands on her hips.

"It is the only way for now."

"What about Kayla?" Birdie asked.

"Mary will see her safe."

Ben and Birdie exchanged glances.

Two more Beguines emerged from one of the bungalows and began making their way across the courtyard toward them. Their long robes made it seem as if they were floating along the ground.

"We have to go," Henri said, urgency filling his voice as he motioned for Birdie and Ben to follow him. "They know me."

They made their way swiftly from the park, following the canal back to the house with the red and purple flowers.

Ben and Birdie followed Henri up the stairs to the front porch and watched anxiously as he fitted an old key in the large lock. It twisted several times and then clicked. He pushed the door open.

A moment later they were back in the dimly lit foyer, greeted by the now familiar fragrance of dust and wood smoke.

"*Merci. Merci beaucoup.* Thank you," Ben said. "Thank you for coming back. I don't know how I would have got out of there otherwise."

"With your card playing skills, it looked like," Birdie said as she examined a tear in her jacket sleeve.

Ben laughed, but there was no humor in it. "I was teaching them to play. I was buying time. It made me useful."

"Thank goodness for those French classes."

Ben nodded. "Yeah. If my parents only knew." He turned to Henri. "*Desole.* I'm sorry. I lost your book."

Henri was about to answer when a pleasant voice startled them from the sitting room.

"Do you mean this book?"

Kayla.

She and Mary were sitting in a soft patch of sunlight in

front of the fireplace working on their dust masterpieces. She held the leather volume up with her free hand.

Mary grinned.

"Kayla!" Birdie ran into the room. "You got out!"

"Yes I did." She smiled. "With Mary's help of course."

"How did you get the book?" Ben asked, not bothering to hide his surprise as he followed Birdie into the room.

"Hmmm," Kayla said, exchanging a knowing glance with Mary. "Let's just say that I encouraged Eva to hand it over."

She held up her right hand to show off her bloodstained knuckles.

"That's awesome!" Ben said, his crooked smile lighting up his battered face.

"Mary helped, of course."

The little girl leaned into Kayla for a quick hug.

"Well, it is done then," Henri said, letting out a tired breath.

They were all quiet for a moment.

"What will you do now?" Birdie asked.

Henri made his way across the room. He stopped beside Mary.

"We will leave Bruges. Soon."

He looked past the dusty lace sheers that covered the parlor windows to the canal beyond, as if he were planning his route.

"Very soon," he continued. "As soon as it is safe. I have my father's maps. He has friends in Venice. He told me to take Mary there if anything ever happened to *Maman*."

Mary looked down at her drawing.

"That is a long journey," Ben said.

"Oui," Henri agreed. "But we are prepared."

"I guess you'll be needing this," Kayla said, holding the book up to him.

He reached out his hand.

As his fingers grasped the corner of the leather-bound book, a loud blast of a taxi horn sounded just outside the window.

"What the hell?" Ben said, as Birdie let out a small scream. Kayla jumped, too.

The taxi had startled them all.

Except for Henri and Mary.

They were gone.

"Birdie..." Kayla began, but her next words died in her throat.

The room around them had changed. Instead of dusty bare floors and sheet-covered furniture, a lovely storyteller carpet lay beneath a love seat and two armchairs. A porcelain tea set sat on a low coffee table between them.

"Whaaa?" Kayla said, regaining her voice. Behind her, the plain brick mantle was now a carved work of art. "What the hell just happened?"

Ben chuckled and Birdie burst out laughing.

"We did it," he said, holding up his hand to high-five Birdie.

She smacked her hand against his. "We sure did. Now let's get the heck out of here before Mrs. Winggen comes home."

Birdie offered a hand to help Kayla up. "Thank you for getting the book. I'm glad you came today. We couldn't have done this without you."

"No problem," Kayla replied, averting her eyes as she gripped Birdie's hand.

Birdie thought they may have been filling with tears.

Kayla dropped Birdie's hand and wiped at the back of her dusty shorts. She stared at the place where Mary had drawn pictures with her only moments before. "I'm think I'm gonna miss that kid."

"She will never forget you," Birdie said. "I'm sure of it."

"We need to go," Ben said, leading the way back into the

foyer. "The last thing we need is to get caught here."

As they left the sitting room, Birdie checked to make sure that nothing looked out of place.

"Birdie, come on," Ben said. He was already standing by the front door. Kayla stood beside him.

"Okay, okay, I was just..." Birdie stepped into the foyer and stopped dead.

"Ben. Look."

There, in the center of the small antique accent table, lay a leather-bound volume with a faded knight embossed on its worn cover.

"He forgot..." Kayla began.

"No," Birdie said. She gently opened the cover and looked at the ancient handwritten script on the brittle paper. "He remembered."

Before you leave Bruges,
take one last stroll around
its peaceful back streets and
imagine what it must have
been like to live here
during its golden age.

Marty McEntire's
Europe for Americans Travel Guide

CHAPTER TWENTY-EIGHT

Birdie, Ben and Kayla made sure that the heavy front door at Witte Beertje Huis was pulled tight and locked behind them.

The morning mist had cleared, making way for a beautiful afternoon. A fresh batch of tourists meandered along the cobblestone lanes, pausing to photograph the sparkling canal, the colorful stepping-stone roofs, and the towering Gothic spires.

A warm breeze lifted the dark hair from Birdie's shoulders as they walked silently through the crowd. Every so often someone would point at them, but no one said a thing.

They followed the sweep of the lane that bordered the canal, and then, for the last time, turned down the alley that would lead them to t'Bruges Huis and back to their normal, ordinary lives.

Above them, a chorus of wood pigeons called to one another as they rustled from rooftop to rooftop of the tightly packed houses.

When they neared the front door of t'Bruges Huis, Birdie

checked her watch.

12:55 pm.

She laughed and held up her wrist to show Ben and Kayla the face of her watch.

They were on time. She couldn't believe it. After everything that happened that morning it was a miracle they weren't late.

They made their way up the wide steps to the front door, the three of them side by side. Birdie punched in the code on the green pad. The door buzzed then clicked open. Ben held it and then followed them into the foyer and onto the mosaic tiles.

As the door latched behind them, the out-of-tune bells at the nearby church began to chime.

"What in holy hell happened to you?" boomed Uncle Noah, bolting up from the armchair he'd been sitting in. Kayla's grandparents were on the love seat and Mrs. Blessing was in the other chair.

They'd pulled a third armchair from the foyer for Mrs. Winggen. Birdie had completely forgotten she was there.

Ben's swollen, blood-streaked face twisted in surprise at his uncle's reaction. Then Birdie saw understanding creep across his deep brown eyes. He turned to examine himself in the foyer mirror.

He grinned broadly and his features contorted like a mask. He touched the thin cut under his eye where Jan had punched him. His face was crusted with trickles of dried blood and the ripped pocket of his shorts hung limp against his leg.

"Guess I should have cleaned myself up," he said sheepishly.

"Yes, you probably should have," Uncle Noah said, putting his hands on his nephew's shoulders and standing behind him so they both reflected in the mirror. Ben winced. Birdie had a feeling he had a bruise or two on his shoulders, too.

"So I'll ask you again. What the hell happened? Did you wreck the bikes?" He glanced up at Birdie and Kayla's reflections in the mirror. "Into each other?"

Ben shook his head.

Mrs. Blessing had reached Birdie by then and cupped her face gently in her hands. "Are you okay? Where have you been? Is that a ... bruise on your forehead?" She reached out instinctively and brushed her cool fingers along the lump. Birdie flinched.

"Kayla?" Mr. Hinnershitz said as he and Mrs. Hinnershitz shuffled into the foyer. "What's the meaning of all this? Your clothes and hands are filthy. Do we need to call the police?"

"Did that boy do this to you?" Mrs. Blessing asked. "The one you were searching for?"

"I sure hope the other guy looks worse," Uncle Noah said, eyeing his nephew's face.

"They do." Birdie said.

Everyone shifted to stare at her.

"They?" Mrs. Blessing repeated.

There were several beats of silence and then Kayla said, "Ben and Birdie got into a tussle with some tourists who were trying to steal the boy's book."

"Ah ha. So you found him then," came a lilting voice from the parlor.

Birdie disengaged herself from her mother and approached Mrs. Winggen. Ben and Kayla followed her.

"We did, Mrs. Winggen," Birdie said, lowering herself to the carpet beside the old woman's chair. Kayla and Ben sat down, too. "His name was Henri. We found his little sister, Mary, too."

Mrs. Winggen looked at them curiously with her deeply hooded blue eyes, sizing them up before she spoke.

"And the book?"

"Henri…" Birdie paused. "We returned it to Henri."

"It was safely in his hands? You are sure?"

"Yes, ma'am," Ben said.

"Very well," Mrs. Winggen said, supporting her slight weight on the arms of the chair as she stood. "Then I suppose it is gone for good."

Ben, Birdie and Kayla exchanged glances.

"I think it may turn up again," Birdie said.

Mrs. Winggen winked at them. "I think you may be right, dear."

"Mrs. Winggen was telling us that she thought the book might be a family heirloom," Mrs. Hinnershitz said. "It's been lost for many years."

"Yes," Mrs. Winggen said, her face growing soft as if she were pulling a memory from a far away place. "I'd seen it only once, when I was a girl, and that was in the library of the old Begijnhof. I asked about it many years later, but by then the sisters said it disappeared. I'd forgotten all about it until you joined me for tea yesterday and showed me the book you found in the Minnewater. I couldn't be sure, of course, but I thought it might be the same book, a book about playing chess, a rare copy. But that wasn't why it was so special to my father."

"Tucked inside," she continued, "sewn in with thick threads, were the handwritten pages of a journal."

Ben and Birdie exchanged glances.

"According to my father, it belonged to my great-grandfather many times over, Henri LeFort. He had written about a journey he took to Venice with his young sister and their time there. He'd followed in his own dead father's footsteps, apparently, and made a fortune as a merchant. He returned to Bruges as a young man and claimed his father's home. My home."

"Witte Beertje Huis," Birdie said.

Mrs. Winggen nodded.

"What a coincidence that the boy you met was also named Henri," Mrs. Hinnershitz said.

"Yes," Mrs. Winggen agreed, winking at them again. "Quite a coincidence indeed."

She lifted her head and walked slowly across the parlor to the foyer.

The children stood.

"It looks like the mystery is solved and your children are home," Mrs. Winggen said, nodding in turn at Mrs. Blessing, Uncle Noah, and the Hinnershitzes. "I shall take my leave. It was a pleasure to meet you all. I wish you safe travels. Please thank Mrs. Devon for the tea."

The adults said their farewells and stepped aside to let Mrs. Winggen pass. Uncle Noah opened the door for her and offered his arm for support.

"Are you okay getting home?" he asked as they descended the steps quite slowly. "I could call you a taxi."

"Yes, young man, I can manage. I have walked these lanes for more than eighty-three years." She paused and made sure he was listening. "And those taxi drivers are crazy. You'd do well to remember that."

"Yes, ma'am," he said. She slipped her hand from his arm.

Uncle Noah watched her until she turned up the alley, then came back into the foyer and closed the door.

All eyes turned to Birdie, Ben, and Kayla who stood together as a motley crew in the sitting room.

"You should really be punished for what you've been doing the past few days," Mrs. Blessing said.

Birdie started to protest but Uncle Noah spoke first.

"I agree," he said, stepping forward until he stood next to Mrs. Blessing. Ben made a sound but Uncle Noah held up a hand to silence him. "However, the Blessings are leaving this afternoon and we're staying in Belgium for a couple more days before we head to Berlin." He looked at Mr. Hinnershitz.

"We're leaving in the morning," he said, his white mustache wiggling as he spoke. He leveled his gaze at Kayla. "Bright and early."

"Okay, okay," she said. "I'll set the alarm on my phone." She patted the pocket of her jean shorts to make sure it was still there, but she didn't take it out.

"So," Uncle Noah continued, "your adventures together appear to be over."

Birdie dropped her head and stared at her sneakers to hide the tears that had leapt unbidden to her eyes. She didn't dare to look at Ben or Kayla.

"You all look exhausted," Mrs. Blessing said. "And you're filthy. Birdie, go up and get yourself cleaned up and then grab your things. We need to be at the car rental shop in half an hour. We'll have to grab lunch on the road. Mrs. Devon has been more than gracious allowing us to keep the room so late on our check-out day."

Birdie shuffled forward. Ben and Kayla followed her up the stairs. The adults moved back into the sitting room and began to speak in low voices.

When they reached the first landing Birdie stopped.

"So, I guess this is it," she said, breaking the silence that was beginning to build.

"I guess," Ben said.

"Where are you going next?" Kayla asked.

"I have no idea," Birdie said. Then she thought for a moment. "Germany, I guess my mom said. Something about castles. But she didn't mention Berlin."

She hadn't paid much attention to all the planning. Where they were going seemed irrelevant back then compared to the fact that they were leaving home at all.

"Bet it won't be as much fun as Bruges," Ben said, a

crooked grin breaking out over his face.

They all laughed.

"Definitely not," Birdie said. She paused, not wanting to leave her new friends behind. "Well, I guess I should go. Get cleaned up."

Kayla opened her arms and Birdie stepped into them. They hugged and then Birdie turned to Ben.

"Stay out of trouble," she said.

"Never," he said. "Bye Birdie."

She walked slowly down the hall to the flight of stairs that would lead to the attic room for the last time.

"Hey, Birdie," Ben called after her.

"Yes?" She stopped and turned back to look at them.

"Do you still have the aventurine?"

Birdie reached into her jacket pocket. She'd completely forgotten about it in all of the excitement.

She pulled it from her pocket. It was cool on her fingers. She held it out for the others to see. They came closer to examine her outstretched hand.

The coppery glass was sparkling with golden flakes.

"The knight is gone," Ben said.

"So is the bear," Kayla said.

Birdie turned the aventurine over on her palm. That side was filled with sparkles, too.

She rubbed it but nothing happened. The flakes didn't swirl and the temperature didn't change.

"Great souvenir," Kayla said.

"Did you know that in French the word *souvenir* means 'memory'?" Ben asked.

Birdie slipped the aventurine back into her pocket and smiled at Ben and Kayla.

"Then I will be sure to never forget you," she said. "Or this magical place."

ABOUT THE AUTHOR

Heidi English loves to travel, study history, and write stories. When she's home, she's based in Pennsylvania. When she's not home, she spends time exploring beautiful places, both in the United States and abroad.

www.birdieabroad.com